CHARMING THE TROLL'S HEART

TROLLKIN LOVERS BOOK FOUR

LYONNE RILEY

Introduction

Stolen from her bed in the middle of the night, Rimi is shipped across the ocean to a strange land and kept in a cage like an animal. She's almost given up hope for escape when a good-natured, roguish troll is assigned to be her new caretaker.

Lo'zar is a petty criminal, smuggling illicit goods from one place to another while enjoying his life as a carefree player. But when he's tasked with transporting a human woman to a buyer, he wonders if he's really doing the right thing.

As Lo'zar grows fond of the clever, sweet Rimi, he knows he has to help her—even if freeing her means putting his life on the line. Can they survive the dangers of the jungle together and get Rimi back home?

Content Warnings

- Graphic depictions of sex
- Abduction and trafficking
- Captive FMC

- Neglect and abuse
- Thoughts of death
- Moderate violence
- On-page death (by gun and sword)
- Claustrophobia
- Crime/thieving/smuggling
- Sexual harassment
- Drug use (off-page)
- Animal death
- Breeding
- Pregnancy
- Birth

CHAPTER 1

Lo'zar

I have too many skeletons in my closet to be messing with lawmen, so when the Attirex city guard comes and questions me about my connections to the underworld, I can't get out soon enough. Nobody wants that kind of attention, especially not me.

The boss sent me ahead to scope out some of the more... unsavory elements in Attirex, one of the few neutral cities that exist between human and trollkin kind. He thought we could open up a new trade channel, perhaps even to humans. There are criminals everywhere regardless of which side you're on, and we all want the same thing: coin. So I came here to find out if the promise of money could expand the clan's reach to the inhospitable desert, because more coin for the clan means more coin for me. With enough money there's no scrounging up leftover bread crusts and picking discarded bones clean. Any meal I could want is within reach.

Then a few weeks back, this human man who spoke poor Trollkin tried to sell me some green salt, the kind of shit that makes you lose your mind when you snort it, just for a while. Long enough to make trouble and maybe get killed.

I turned him away, of course. The boss's operation has no need for the green. Trading in salt is a great way to end up executed or rotting away in prison the rest of your life.

But it doesn't matter whether or not I'm innocent. I've accidentally attracted the attention of the city guard—the captain, no less—and I can't have her looking any deeper into me, just in case she finds the inevitable dirt.

I still can't believe it. I fucked a human. Me, a troll, fucked a *human*. I'd never been given the gift before, or frankly, even considered it, but now I'm certifiably changed. It will be hard to want anything else after putting my cock inside that tiny, hot cunt, stroking in and out of her while I enjoyed her soft features and big, bouncing breasts.

I'll never forget it as long as I live.

Unfortunately, the captain I fucked and her orc buddy showed up at the tavern where I'd been scoping prospects, and interrogated me about possibly-illegal goings-on. The guy trying to sell me salt had been offed, and they were searching for a connection.

Now that I'm in their sights, my cover's blown and I can't finish the job. I hate not completing a mission, but I hop on the first caravan out of town anyway to confess my failure to the boss.

The journey back to Kalishagg is long and arduous, but I'm overjoyed to see my home city again. Kalishagg, the trollkin's biggest city, sits atop a hill above the jungle. The streets are loud and reek of animal, the shops are covered by deer hide canopies, and the windows are barred with iron.

Best of all, there aren't any humans anywhere. I think I've had enough for now.

I visit the mechanic's shop on the far end of town, where my buddy Graz is hammering away at some new gadget of his. He's always inventing new and fascinating stuff. He has a machine that reaches into a box full of rats and feeds one to his pet lizard every couple of days. Once he built a portable fire that's supposed to cook your meat for you, but it always burns mine.

When I walk in, Graz turns a tiny crank to reel his microscope into his goggles, then pushes them up onto his head. "You're back early," he says, waving. "Thought you'd be gone for a few months."

"Things didn't go as expected," I say. There are some new maps up on Graz's wall. He's been "investigating local legends" lately, which really just means tacking up some paper, drawing a big map on it and marking red dots in random places. There's even one very close by, out in the jungle. My friend has always been the curious sort, ever since we were whelps living on the street. I was the one who made sure we always had food to eat while he fiddled and experimented with whatever leftover bits of machinery he could find.

"'Didn't go as expected'?" Graz says, arching an eyebrow. "That sounds ominous."

I have so much to tell him after getting ratted out in Attirex. He's been my best friend since I saved him from getting run over by an oxcart, so if I can tell anyone about the human cunt, it's him. He'll be amazed by it—and probably a little horrified.

But I have to report to the boss first. I head for the door on the far end of the shop and pull a lever. The elevator rattles to life, another of Graz's inventions.

"I've gotta run," I say. "Let's get a beer later."

Graz nods and slides his goggles back over his eyes, then begins soldering some metal, sending sparks flying. The elevator opens and I step inside.

It's a long, rickety trip down into the caves below Kalishagg. Almost nobody knows these gaping crystal caverns are here, right under the city, which is fortunate for us. It's the perfect place to base our operations and house all our coin and stolen goods.

When the elevator reaches the bottom, I have to really tug to get the door to open. Kugara, a spry orcess, jumps to her feet when I step out.

"Lo'zar! You're back!" She's the youngest member of the clan and a little green still. *Ha, ha.* There's extra shine in her eyes today as she ducks out of the store room to greet me. "Didn't expect you so soon. It's a nice surprise, though." She tucks a lock of her thick black hair behind one ear and bats her eyelashes.

A month ago, I probably would have propositioned her. Taken her to bed. Made her scream my name. But after my tryst with the captain of the guard, I can't see anything in her that I desire—just another peon who wants to impress the boss, same as the rest of us.

"Hey, Kugara," I say with a salute.

"Did you find anything?" she asks.

I sigh. "Gotta report to Gusak first, then I'll catch you up."

"Right, right. Well, go on. He's in the pit watching a fight."

I head down the first flight of stairs, which are really just steps carved into stone. Don't want to slip or you'll go tumbling down into a comfy nest of sharp crystal stalagmites.

When I say the caverns are big, I'm understating it. The main one is hundreds of feet from top to bottom, and covered in blue, green and purple crystals that jut out in every direction. It spirals off into additional cave systems that are perfect for storage and living space. I, personally, cannot wait to sleep in my own bed again, assuming no one else has taken it over while I was away.

On my way down to the lower levels, I pass caverns full of weapons with jeweled hilts, priceless paintings, even a red velvet armchair with solid teak legs. There are exotic animals, which Kugara cares for, and a collection of stolen artifacts from some long-forgotten ruin.

It's when I reach the cavern typically reserved for raw supplies —gold ingots, reams of silk, and fine furs—that I see it: a rather large cage now occupies half the space. That's odd. I have to pause and peer close to see what's inside.

It's a human. A *woman*. She's mostly naked, only a few strips of rags clinging to her body, and she's utterly filthy. When I approach, she retreats to the far back of her cage where she bumps into an overflowing chamberpot. It all reeks of shit and piss.

I don't understand what I'm seeing. What is a human doing here, being kept in a cage like one of Graz's rats? We keep some animals in cages, exotic creatures to be sold to wealthy buyers. But never a person. Never a human. My gut twists.

She might be one of them, but she's still a sentient creature.

My eyes land on hers. The woman's irises are a piercing gray, almost silver, and deeper than the sea. I almost stumble on the steps, which would certainly be a fatal mistake, so I pause briefly to stabilize myself. I can't help looking at her again, and taking in her huge, frightened eyes, her flared nostrils, her pink lips carved into a scowl. Her black hair is dirty and matted to her head.

There's no time for this. The boss will want to know what went down in Attirex, and why I failed to secure any new contacts there. Hopefully I'll be forgiven for getting sniffed out by the city guard before I could make any real progress.

But as I continue on down the stairs, I can't stop thinking about the woman in the cage. The worst part was that it felt like she had looked inside me, right to the core of me. All I want to know is what she saw.

RIMI

I don't know how long it's been since I was taken from my bed in the middle of the night by shadowy creatures with great big tusks. Back then I was accustomed to my huge, plush mattress, my piles of pillows, and my downy comforter. Maybe life in my family's big house was often tense and cold, but at least I was safe there, with hot food every day and even an outhouse. Now all I know is the hard floor of my cage and the ratty blanket I've been given to keep my shivers at bay.

First the creatures shipped me across the ocean, my feet tied and my body shoved inside of a wooden crate with holes for breathing and a slot for food. I refused the food at first, until my stomach became a painful, empty pit and I was forced to take the dried meat offered through the slot. It was a long trip full of awful swaying, and I had to try my hardest not to throw up. I often failed. My waste was removed occasionally and fresh straw put in, but otherwise I lived in my own excrement. I cried myself to sleep more times than not, wondering if I'd see home, or even the light of day, ever again. Had my parents been taken, too?

No. If they were, they'd have been there in that ship's hold with me. Whoever stole me, I was the only one they wanted.

Once we reached our destination, my crate was taken off the ship and loaded onto a cart that bumped and banged over uneven ground. I caught glimpses of sunlight through the vent, but that was only for the briefest of moments before I descended into the darkness again. I clawed at the holes and cried out, hoping someone would take pity on me, but no one did. Someone barked at me in a guttural language I couldn't understand, and rattled the crate, sending me smashing into one of the walls. I've kept quiet ever since.

When the lid was finally opened, I had never felt such relief—but it was short-lived. I was dragged from the crate and shoved into a metal cage, like an animal, and the door was bolted shut. I wondered if it would ever unbolt again.

Only then did I finally get a good look at my captors: huge creatures with four fingers on each hand, and tusks protruding from their mouths that curve up into dangerous points. Their skin comes in various colors, from green to bright blue and purple. They have pointed ears and hideous faces.

When I saw a trollkin for the first time, the last of my hope vanished. I'm never going home.

I'm certain that's what they are. Trollkin are monsters that exist only in stories back in Yusala, in the fairy tales and legends we tell. We were once a single civilization, the origin of all sentient life on our world. In the time of magic, war overtook our people and we divided into humans and trollkin: one majestic, and one barbaric. Where humans were venerated, the trollkin were given monstrous forms and terrible, big tusks as punishment for their vicious, violent ways.

I never imagined that I'd meet one in person. They lived on the big continent, a place that had always seemed oh so far away—almost made-up. But now I'm here as their prisoner, and they are most certainly real.

I don't know how long I've been in this cage, shoved into one of many small caves along the walls of a huge cavern that's filled to the brim with brightly-colored crystals. It would be beautiful if the situation were different. The stone almost glows, like there's magic inside.

A young female trollkin with bright green skin has been tasked with bringing me food and water and occasionally emptying out my chamberpot. Once I tried to talk to her, to beg her to free me, but she ignored me as she did her duties. She clearly resents having to care for me, and I resent her in return for being one of the monsters who stole me from my home, who hold me captive like a beast, feeding me just enough to keep me alive.

Occasionally, more of the creatures come and go along the stairs that span the cavern, taking them right past my cage. None of them pay attention to me as they go. I don't know how much time has passed when I see *him*.

He's the blue kind of trollkin with the longer tusks, though his skin carries a purplish hue. He's young and his eyes are bright, and he walks with a confident swagger down the steps that pass my cage. But unlike the others, he stops walking when he passes, and our eyes connect. He studies me as I study him. Something about him is strangely familiar, as if I've looked into his orange-red eyes before. Though he quickly starts walking away, I have a feeling that I'll see him again.

Lo'zar

The boss is not as upset as I'd feared when I recount my story, twisting the rings on my hands with barely-disguised nerves. Gusak hasn't built his empire out of terror, like many do in our line of work. He listens to reason, relying on us to provide good information and assess risks. But he's also a powerful orc in and of himself, and still capable of inflicting awful punishments on those who wrong him. I would never cross Gusak unless I wanted to die with my hands and feet chewed off by alligators.

"It was good you left before you were apprehended," Gusak says, not taking his eyes off of the fight happening in front of us. One huge, scarred orc grabs a smaller troll by the waist and hefts him high over his head, then smashes his opponent into the floor. Naturally, I will not mention my dalliance with the human captain of the guard. That was incredibly foolish—though I don't regret doing it one bit.

"Perhaps there is too much turmoil at the moment in Attirex," Gusak goes on. "I will look elsewhere to expand our operations."

This is why he's the boss, of course. He's the one constantly looking for opportunity and seizing it when it's safe to do so. Rarely does he leave himself vulnerable or exposed.

"Thank you for trusting my judgment," I say, pleased that he's letting me off the hook so easy. He's not one to punish when the circumstances are outside our control, but I thought he'd be more disappointed in me. He just nods, then lets out a guffaw when the orc in the pit lands a heavy blow.

As I turn to leave, I hear Gusak say, "Lo'zar, before you go. I have a new job for you to do."

A new job, after I failed this one? I turn around and nod quickly, eager to make up for my mistake. "Sure, boss. Whatever you want."

He picks up his mug of beer and swirls it around, finally sparing me a glance. "You might have seen my new acquisition on your way down."

"The human?" I ask, shifting uncomfortably when I remember the small woman living in her own waste, and how quiet and terrified she was.

"We're transporting her to a buyer. And you'll be overseeing her."

Overseeing her…? He can't mean what I think he means. Tending to the human's needs is Kugara's job. Not that she's put much effort into it so far.

If he's giving me a newbie's work, perhaps he's not actually forgiven me for Attirex.

"O-oh. All right." I must have to redeem myself to him. You get ahead in Gusak's eyes by doing what he says and doing it well, without question. "Will do, boss."

Gusak nods once, and I take my cue to leave. On my way back up stairs, I pass other trollkin making their way to their rooms, the bath, or the fire pit. I come to a stop in front of the cage with the human inside.

The woman is sleeping, a torn bit of leather partially covering her like a blanket. I wonder why Gusak has her, and who's intending to buy her. I'm surprised, too. Smuggling goods is one thing, but smuggling humans?

I didn't think that was the sort of work we did. My stomach roils just looking at her, curled up in a shivering ball.

I'm certainly not going to deal with that stink for an entire trip, so the first thing I do is find Kugara. "You've been letting that human live in her own filth?" I demand.

"What do you expect me to do?" She shoves a handful of nuts into her mouth, chewing loudly. "Cleaning and bathing humans is above my pay grade."

How someone this lazy became part of a crime syndicate, I'll never know. "Well, apparently it is exactly my pay grade," I say. "Gusak's moving her somewhere, and I'm taking over for you." The least we could do is empty the human's waste bucket.

Kugara shrugs. "She's all yours. Good luck."

CHAPTER 2

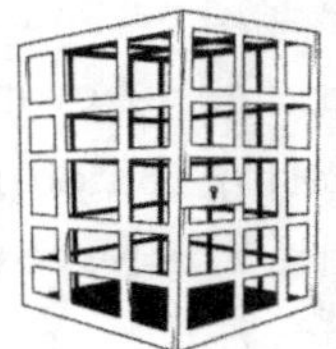

RIMI

The next day, the trollkin with the purplish-blue skin, bright eyes, and swagger returns. Short, wild hair shoots out on top of his head and a huge, thick braid trails down his back. He gestures a lot with his hands when he talks, which are all decorated with jeweled rings, and his gold necklaces clink whenever he moves. Naturally, I can't understand anything he's saying. That's how it's been since I was put in this cage—the monsters constantly talking about me, throwing words in their strange language at me, and then growing angry when I don't obey their commands.

This is hell, and I will never escape.

When this new trollkin opens my cage, I retreat as far into the back corner as I can. I'm not letting another one of those monsters get their grubby hands on me if I can help it. He uses a soothing voice as he reaches inside and grabs the edge of my chamber pot, then grimaces as he removes it. I think it's the first time in a week that anyone's bothered to empty it out.

Is he my new prison guard? Great. A new master to taunt me through the bars and feed me barely enough scraps to live on. He might not have the same hatred etched onto his face as the green female, but he's dangerous all the same.

Later he brings the chamber pot back, and, with it, a thicker blanket. He holds it out to me, but I crawl even further back, pressing myself against the cold bars on the other side of the cage. Realizing I'm not going to budge, he drops the blanket near me and closes the door again, muttering something. Then he's gone.

I let out a relieved breath. The less attention on me, the better. At first, when they put me in this cage, I fought. I rattled the bars and cried for help, hoping someone would take pity on me and let me out. But the monsters only shook my cage, sending me sprawling against the cold metal bars. They taunted me and threw food at me. Since then I strive to be as uninteresting as possible.

Sometimes, though, I consider making a ruckus again. Perhaps if I bit and kicked and tried to run for it, they would give up and kill me. That is, perhaps, my only chance of ever reaching freedom from this horrid, stinking, miserable place. If it meant this would end, I would happily let them slit my throat—but they seem more interested in keeping me just on the edge of life.

Often I wonder what they have planned for me. There must be some goal in all this, but I can't fathom what that is besides torturing me.

Once I'm alone, I reach out for the blanket this latest prison guard has given me, only to find it's soft and sturdy under my hands. I'm surprised I would be given something of this quality. It will surely keep me warm tonight. I don't think I've felt warm in weeks—maybe even months. I truly have no concept of how long I was on that ship, or how long I've been trapped in this cage.

Now that my chamber pot isn't overflowing anymore, I can smell the scent baked into the fabric when I wrap myself up in it. It's just faintly musky, like someone uses it often. I wonder if it belongs to the trollkin who gave it to me. I inhale the smell again, because something about it is comforting, an emotion I haven't experienced since this whole ordeal began. The scent reminds me of sunlight. Who knows how long it's been since I felt sun on my skin? Before I was always outdoors, soaking in its warmth as I went on an afternoon horseback ride or swam in the lake nearby. Often it was to escape my parents' bickering, but the sun's warm rays also gave me life.

The scent of those blissful days in my nose, I fall asleep, and for the first time in a while I don't cry.

Unfortunately, this small spark of hope is quickly extinguished. Not only do I have a new overseer, but the trollkin are planning to move me.

When the wooden crate appears, I scream. It's uncontrollable. I can't be shoved in there again, I just can't. I will stop breathing until I choke. Every inch of my skin is pulling me away.

The trollkin from last night appears at the door to my cage, and again he uses his soothing voice on me, but I won't have it. I crawl into the very back corner of my cage, trying to stay as far from the crate as possible. He reaches in to grab me, and I lash and bite at him because I won't go. This time, I will fight to the death.

But I'm much smaller than he is, and when the creature's big hands wrap around my wrists, he drags me across the floor of the cage without much trouble. It looks like he wants to be here even less than I do. Then the mouth of the crate looms in front of me like a sea monster's great maw, and I scream and scream until there's no air left in my lungs. The female trollkin and my new prison guard work together to shove me into the crate and seal the top, so I'm trapped once more.

When the light goes out, I fall on my back and sob.

LO'ZAR

This human is clearly traumatized. Beyond traumatized. When she sees the crate come out, her eyes go as big as marbles, and she lets out a shrill, terrified scream. She screams the entire time as we force her into the crate, fighting with everything she has in her small body, but we're bigger and stronger. It's no contest.

I feel filthy as she sobs inside the crate. Kugara wipes her hands off on her pants. "Ew," she says. "She's disgusting." I don't point out the fact the human is only dirty and gross because no one here has been taking care of her properly.

Instead, I ask, "How long does she stay in the crate?"

"Until we get out of town. Once we're out in the jungle we'll put her back in the cage." She winks at me, and I don't like the look in her eye. "Don't you worry." She thinks I have some scheme in mind for the little human, and that concerns me. I've caused plenty of fights in my life by hopping from one bed to the next, and the last thing I need is for her to get jealous.

Thankfully, we won't be alone on our journey, as another orc— a big idiot named Drozeg—is coming along with us for security. He's just a pile of beef, really. I would be much more effective against any attacking animal or trollkin with my sword or gun. I keep one of each on me, because you never know what sort of trouble you'll end up in and I like to be prepared.

The human doesn't stop crying as we carry the crate upstairs into the elevator. We load up the wagon along with the cage, filling the rest of it with dry goods and supplies, like we're headed out on a hunt. Taking a living human out of the city would raise far too many questions, and Gusak likes to keep questions at a minimum. This should get past the city guard without too much fuss.

Then Drozeg sits down on the back of the wagon, on top of the crate with the woman in it, and I hope he doesn't suffocate her. At least we can't hear her crying anymore, but I can't stop picturing her inside that crate, packed in so tight she can't even move. I'm tense for the rest of the ride through town, until we arrive at the huge gates that lead out of Kalishagg and into the jungle.

I don't know exactly where we're headed, but I know that it's north—far north. Only Kugara has the map. Once we get there, it'll be up to me to deliver the human to the buyer and extract our payment.

Who buys a human woman? I can only imagine what disgusting things they have planned for her, and it sends a shiver down my spine. I wanted to ask, but I also don't want to appear too interested in Gusak's business. We're just the executors of his will, and questions that don't pertain to that execution are superfluous. They only draw unnecessary attention.

We get in line at the guard station and wait until it's our turn to declare. Goods headed in and out of the city must be checked and taxed, but we're just "going out to capture rare animals" and we'll pay the tax when we return. Luckily, the human has given up fighting for now, so no one is the wiser as to our true cargo.

"Next!" the guard calls out, and our wagon rolls through the gates without earning a second glance.

Once we're out of earshot, I growl at Drozeg to get off the crate's small vent. "We don't want her to die before she reaches the buyer." With a grunt of annoyance, he finds a new place to sit.

When it feels like we've traveled far enough, I tell Kugara to take us off the main road. Hidden from sight, I hop down from the wagon and head to the crate in the back. I made sure before we left that the human had a fresh, clean chamberpot, and another blanket she can lie on. Now she'll have one on each side of her when she sleeps.

We pry off the lid of the crate, and the little woman is so shocked that she doesn't move at first. Then, when she realizes she's in the fresh, outside air, she claws and flails, trying to worm her way past us. But Drozeg simply grabs her around the waist and stuffs her into the open door of the cage like a chicken, and she cries out as the blunted edges leave their marks. I cringe at the sound.

"Let me handle the human from now on," I say, shoving him out of the way as I close the door and bolt it. "You're going to damage her." The big lout just rolls his eyes and climbs back up on the wagon.

It's time to go. As we set off, though, something in my chest squeezes tight. Something is off with this mission, wrong, and I don't like it.

CHAPTER 3

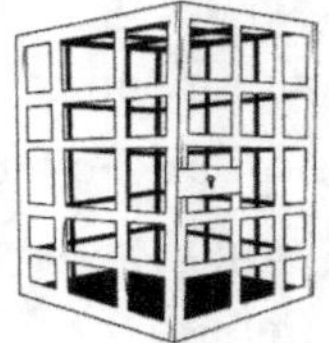

RIMI

I never thought I would be relieved to return to my cage, but anything is better than that horrible crate. I want to throw it into a fire and burn it and then stomp on the ashes.

Upon the door bolting closed, however, I'm puzzled to find yet another new blanket waiting for me. Compared to the ratty thing I had before, this feels like luxury. Decadence. As the wagon resumes moving, I put one blanket underneath me so my bare legs aren't chafing on the metal floor, then roll the other one around me to cover my half-naked body.

That's not the only enhancement to my living conditions. Now we're outside, and my captors have, remarkably, left my cage uncovered. I've never appreciated open sky as much as I do right now. Back home in Yusala, we had a great garden that seemed to go on forever, and I loved to simply stroll through it endlessly.

How far away that life seems now, like a nice dream I had before I was abruptly awoken to this nightmare. Perhaps my parents are rather cold people, but at this moment I miss them immensely. Just thinking about their faces, imagining my home, makes my chest ache with longing. Do they miss me just as much as I miss them?

I can't go to that dark place again. If I let the misery consume me, then I will simply cry and cry until there's nothing left. Instead of ruminating on everything I've lost, I lean my head back against the bars and close my eyes, trying to enjoy the fresh air as much as I can as we bump and jolt along the road. Beyond the edge of the path the jungle is dense and dark, overflowing with ferns so big they look prehistoric, and hanging vines that blot out the sun. It's very much unlike my homeland of big valleys and lakes. The foliage is dense and the air is so thick it's almost wet. Occasionally, I can make out the shapes of square rocks deep in the trees. Are there buildings out there? Ruins of some kind?

A few hours into our journey I hear distant voices, and suddenly the big, mean trollkin with the bright green skin is draping something over the top of my cage to hide me.

Wherever I am now seems to be inhabited only by these monsters. If I scream and raise the alarm, will these other travelers help me? Or will I simply make my situation worse? They could always put me back in the crate.

The thought makes me gag, so I keep quiet while the light disappears and the voices come closer.

My captors and the visitors share a quick exchange, then we're on our way again, bumping along the road. After a while the cloth is removed, and it's the trollkin who gave me the blankets pulling it down. He takes the big green guy's spot next to my cage.

I don't speak or make a sound, not wanting to earn the crate. I won't forget that he shoved me in there, forcing the lid closed on top of me. If I ever got the chance, I would drive a dagger through him the same way I would the green female who let me rot and fester.

After what feels like an hour or two of silence, my jailer leans towards the cage bars and starts to talk to me. It takes me by surprise, someone speaking directly to me and without hatred. I wish I knew what he was saying—in fact, I wish I understood anything that was happening to me. I feel like a marionette a child bashes against the walls of a toy theater.

After a while of him chatting amiably, as if we were old buddies, I realize he's been looking at me intently, waiting for some kind of response.

I shake my head. I have no idea what he's saying. Not that it matters.

He gestures at himself. "Lo'zar," he says. He taps his chest again. "*Arg gak* Lo'zar."

Is he trying to tell me his name? What does he care if I know his name? Still, a submerged desire to communicate, to be heard, flares to life as he pays attention to me. I didn't realize how much I've missed simply speaking with another living creature.

So I decide to indulge him, because even if I can't understand a word he's saying, at least it's something. I repeat the word back to him quietly. "Lo'zar?"

This earns a smile, and he has a rather big one. His wide mouth takes up most of his face, raising his tusks almost up to his eyes, and it's strangely charming.

I shake my head. He is a monster. My captor.

"*Yag gak?*" He points at me this time. "*Yag gak?*"

He wants to know my name now. For a moment, I can't even remember it. It's been so long since I felt human, since I felt like *me*, that my own name is something I have to search for.

"Rimi," I answer finally, pointing at myself. "I'm Rimi."

He tests the word. "Ree-mee?"

Sure. Good enough. I nod my head, and he smiles again. Why is he always smiling at me?

But nothing about this trollkin makes sense. He talks some more at me, occasionally dropping my name to keep me paying attention. He sure likes to talk—and I can't say that I mind the company. After a while he pulls out a bag and fishes for something in it, finally withdrawing a big piece of red fruit I've never seen before.

My mouth waters. Fresh fruit. It would taste incredible. Not that I haven't had fruit before, but now it seems like a lifetime ago. I would give anything for some kind of fresh food. Lo'zar continues talking, occasionally taking a bite. After a while, though, he notices I'm watching his hands with keen interest, and he looks down at the fruit.

He asks me a question, and holds it up. If he's offering me some, my answer is a vehement yes.

"Please," I say, nodding my head and reaching out to it. "Please?"

There's a look of pity in his eyes as he reaches through the bars and hands me the rest of the fruit. It's bigger than my whole hand, and I bite into it with a deep, profound joy. It tastes like everything I could have hoped for and more. It's sweet and tart and perfect, and the cool juice runs down my throat in the most soothing way. It's also dripping down the side of my face, but I'm too engrossed in this incredible meal to pay attention to it. I suck down the fruit almost as fast as my stomach can bear, and soon all that's left is the big pit.

When I finally look up at Lo'zar again, he's staring at me with his mouth ajar. Embarrassment sweeps through me thinking of how quickly I ate his food. It just tasted so good. I don't have a napkin, so I wipe my face with one of my filthy sleeves, then I toss the pit through the bars of the cage.

Lo'zar chuckles at this and removes another piece of fruit from his bag. He leans back as he eats this one, propping himself up on his elbow on a box of goods while he watches me. There's a mischievous look in his eyes, and he seems a little full of himself. I don't ask for another piece of the fruit, but when he's almost finished with half, a look of guilt crosses the trollkin's face. He hands me the other half, and I wolf it down a little less vigorously this time.

"Thank you," I say. He just tilts his head—clearly he doesn't understand what I'm saying—so I smile and nod, gesturing at the fruit pit.

Lo'zar's face lights up, and he smiles back. *"Grunag zig."* That must mean, *you're welcome*.

He's being so kind to me, and I'm latching onto it like a plant starved for light.

But why? Why is this one treating me this way, like a person, when the others have tossed their used trash into my cage? Suspicion creeps up my neck.

He must have some plan for me, and I just don't know what it is.

And yet, with a full belly, I lay down on the blanket he gave me, pull the other one up over my nakedness, and fall asleep.

LO'ZAR

I've never, ever gotten turned on just by watching someone eat fruit before.

I mean, plenty of other little things have turned me on. I absolutely love when a female reaches down and touches herself. That's a big one. I've also gotten hard watching someone take off their clothes. Hell, even just bending down and picking something up off the floor can be profoundly erotic. Once, all it took was a trolless's seductive smile.

Never just... eating a piece of fruit. As the rivulets of juice roll down the sides of her small face, I feel my cock getting fat and warm under my pants.

Damn. The human woman—Ree-mee?—might just be a little bit cute. The thought should revolt me. We trollkin have cut down humans for territory as long as our civilizations have existed. We just fought a bloody war, for fuck's sake, but I think I've been twisted. Maybe if you put your cock inside a human once, it's like a disease that takes over, and now here I am lusting over another one.

Ree-mee swallows up the last of the second fruit I gave her like it's the first meal she's had in days. Then she curls up in the blankets, and without any pomp and circumstance, falls asleep.

I find myself staring at her face as the wagon bumps along. She has a small nose, and an equally small, dainty mouth. Her black hair lies in oily tangles all over her head, and I think the poor thing could use a bath.

I work my way up to the front of the wagon and lean over where Kugara is driving the horses. "Hey," I say. "Do you know how long it's going to be to get to the buyer?"

"Better get cozy," is all she says.

I grunt in annoyance. "I'm asking because we should probably get this human cleaned up before we deliver her. We don't know what she's... er, going to be used for."

This piques Kugara's interest. "Do you think she's going to be a kinky sex toy?" she asks. My throat goes dry. What a grotesque thought, some lecherous old orc buying a human woman just to tie her up and abuse her.

"Maybe," I say. "Anyway, she also reeks. It's disgusting."

Kugara sniffs the air, then sighs. "Ugh. You're not wrong about that." Letting the reins drop for a moment, she reaches into her pocket and pulls out a map. There's a red star and a circle around it up near the top, where I assume we'll find the buyer. She traces her finger along the line of the road.

"Tomorrow there's a river off that way," she says, gesturing vaguely to the west. "Then you can get her all clean for her new *master*." Kugara giggles at this and picks the reins back up. How can she be so callous about another living thing?

With that settled, I return to the back of the wagon to watch Ree-mee sleep a while longer. When it's time to set up camp, I give her some of my smoked meat rations, and she doesn't hide at the back of the cage this time. She slides close, only for a second, and takes it from my hands. The brush of her tiny fingers over mine sends a shockwave up my arm. Then it's gone, and she's feverishly shoving the food in her mouth and relishing each bite.

That night, I lie in my bedroll thinking about the fruit juice spilling down the sides of her face while she laps it up.

The following day we come to a stop just after a junction, where Kugara guides the horses off the side of the road. "Since you're looking after her, it's on you to wash her," she says. "I'm not gonna be the one to do it just because I'm a girl."

I don't mind that at all. Maybe once Ree-mee is clean, she'll smile at me again.

Speaking of which, she's sitting up in her cage looking around, probably wondering why we've stopped. I go to the door of her cage and open it. She doesn't retreat, but she looks nervous, too. I hold up a rope, and then put my wrists together to mime what I want.

Her eyebrows lower and she backs up a step. Damn. This is not going to be easy, and I don't want to have to drag her out again. Once more I gesture for her to give me her hands, and then point out into the trees. I try to mime washing as best I can, scrubbing under my armpits and running my hand up over my hair. Bathing is a little sexy, so I put my best effort into mimicking what a nice bath would look like.

I stop when I hear laughter. The human is watching me,

covering her mouth, her eyes lit up with humor. When I gesture for her hands again she offers them to me, though I don't think she yet understands what I'm taking her to do.

Once she's tied up, I wrap the other end of the rope around my wrist and lead her out of the cage. I pick her up and jump down from the wagon, and she lets out a little shriek of surprise.

"Don't sully the goods," Kugara calls out to me.

Gross.

I set Ree-mee down on the ground and she looks thunderstruck. I gesture into the woods and pull on the rope. Time to follow me.

She gives me a suspicious look, and digs her feet in. I know I shouldn't be surprised, but I had hoped this would be easier. I tug again, hoping I won't have to pull her along. That certainly won't endear her to me.

Is that what I'm after? Yes. I want her to trust me, to know I'm not like Kugara and Drozeg. I want to deserve that from her. So I crouch down and look up into her eyes.

"Ree-mee?" I say, testing it out. She gives a slight nod, her brow still furrowed. "I'm not going to hurt you. All right?" First I pull out my sword, and she cringes, but I drop it to the ground. My gun goes next. I hold out my open hands, showing her I mean her no harm. The creases in her face soften, and I think I'm getting through. I gesture behind us, off into the jungle. "I promise you'll be happier after a bath."

Finally, after a quick glance back at the wagon, she nods. At least she's out of her cage for a while. I get back to my feet and this time, she follows along dutifully, and I feel a surge of pride. For good measure, though, I pick my gun back up when she's not looking and slip it into my pants.

If I've learned anything in my life scrounging in back alleyways, it's that you should always have a back-up plan.

We press through trees and undergrowth, in the direction that

Kugara told me I could find the river. Then, sure enough, it appears. Vines hang down to the surface, and I catch sight of an animal's head as it slides under the water. I'll have to be careful the little human doesn't get eaten.

Once we're at the riverside, I realize that her hands are bound, and I'll have to take her clothes off myself. But when I approach, she takes a wary step back.

"You're going to bathe," I tell her, pointing at the water. Her eyes widen a little. "Bathe. Not drown."

I hold onto her rope and try to peel her torn rag of a shirt off, but she starts to wriggle and squirm away from me. This is going to be impossible, especially with the rope around her arms. Why did I think this was a good idea again?

It's not like she's got much clothing left to speak of. Her breasts are barely covered, and she's got only one sleeve left. Her pants are torn up to the thigh. I wonder if any of my clothes would fit her, but remember I'm twice her size.

Oh well. That's the best she's going to get. These rags are just as filthy as her body, and there's no point getting her clean just to put them back on and dirty her again.

I pull her against me so she can't squirm free, and lean down to rip through her shirt. She screeches and tries to jerk back, but I don't let her go until I've torn it all the way off. Then I grab her shredded pants and do the same thing, splitting them at the seam. She wriggles and fights and claws, but it has to be done.

Finally, she's naked in front of me, and she's desperately trying to cross her arms over her chest. I have to admit that she's gorgeous, with little round breasts, a narrow waist, and rounded hips. Her skin is like elephant ivory.

I realize that since I'm the one holding her rope, I'm going to have to get in with her. I take off my own shirt and drop it to the ground. Her eyes widen as I unbuckle and pull down my pants.

Unfortunately, I'm starting to respond to her body, so I turn around and get into the water as fast as I can.

Ree-mee lets out a yelp as I wrap my big hands around her sides and plop her into the river next to me. She splashes, trying to get away, so I let her go while keeping her rope tied around my wrist.

"See?" I say, running my hand down my chest in the water, imitating my bathing gesture from before. "Wash."

She finally gets the message. Relief spreads across her face, and I hate to think what she feared. She hastily ducks under the water to get her hair wet, but when she reaches up to clean it, she finds her hands tied.

Shit. I'm going to have to do this for her, aren't I?

Chapter 4

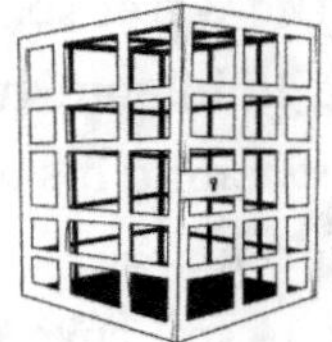

Rimi

The big lunk was trying to tell me to bathe. Oh, how I wish I could understand him, and he could understand me. That would save us both so much headache. And then maybe I could convince him to let me go.

Still, he didn't have to tear all my clothes off that way. I'd been certain something much worse was going to happen than tossing me in the river, especially when I saw that surprisingly large, purple-blue penis hanging between Lo'zar's sculpted legs. It had started to get thick and swollen before he hopped into the water and pulled me in along with him, and I wondered if he meant to use it on me.

But, no, not Lo'zar. Again he mimics bathing, which is really one of the funniest things I've ever seen in my life. I'd thought my prison guard was all big, long arms and legs until I see him naked. I'm fascinated by his chest, filled out with lean muscle, his abdomen divided up into neat, powerful squares. I've seen one or two human men naked, but never someone with Lo'zar's body. He has a sleek line that runs from his hips down to his groin.

I shouldn't be thinking about any of this. All I want is to wash my hair, so I duck under the water to get it wet. But when I reach back to clean it, I find my hands are still bound with rope.

I'm going to need some help.

Lo'zar has crouched in the water so I can't see below his waist. He swims towards me and holds out his hands in a non-threatening gesture, then mimes washing his hair.

Oh. He's going to do it for me.

I don't have much choice, so I turn around and lie back, carefully keeping my breasts below the surface. Then I feel his big hands lift my hair, and he runs his four fingers through it to get the tangles out. I'm surprised at how gentle he is for being such a big creature, and he doesn't tear any out as he washes. I sink into his hands as the sensation of someone touching me with such gentleness lulls my eyes closed.

That's when I feel him against my back—just a soft press right where that big, blue cock would be.

He's turned on by this. By me.

I should be frightened. It's just the two of us here, naked in a river. Me and a big, frightening trollkin, and he's washing my hair with the tip of his cock prodding me. I should worry about where this is going to lead, but he doesn't do anything untoward, and even tries to adjust so he's not touching me. I hear him mutter something in his guttural language, like he's chastising himself, as he continues washing my hair. Then his hands move down to my shoulders, my arms, and my back, making sure to scrub the grime and filth off of every inch of my skin, using one of my rags as a washcloth.

Unconsciously, I start to relax into it, letting my head droop forward while he reaches under the water and washes down my lower back and hips. He hesitates just above my butt, and then seems to decide to skip it and moves on to my legs. When he turns me around, he does the same with my breasts—avoiding them while he scrubs my chest and stomach.

I don't realize that I've become putty in his huge hands until he withdraws them and stands up. Oh. I guess the bath is done now. Almost immediately, I miss the feel of him rubbing me down all over. But when I turn around in the water to thank him... his enormous, hard cock is right in my face.

My feet wheel in surprise. As I try to put some distance between us, my heel catches on a rock I can't see, and I tumble backwards into the river. With my hands tied up, I can't catch myself or fight my way back to the surface. The water closes around my face, then my nose. I let out a panicked yelp that only gets swallowed up.

Above me, I hear Lo'zar shout something, but it's muffled. There's a dark shape moving through the water, *fast*. Before I can even try to get my feet under me, a huge mouth opens and flat, white teeth shine out from inside.

Suddenly, the rope tied around my arms jerks me back, and I'm yanked away from the monster's jaw right as it closes—ripping out some of my hair. It's Lo'zar hauling me up with him, out of the reach of a massive creature with shining brown skin and, admittedly, adorable little ears. The huge beast lets out a bellow, and starts to charge us.

While I gag and cough from the water I swallowed, Lo'zar tucks me under one arm and leaps out of the river. As our attacker clambers up the riverbank, Lo'zar scrambles to get to our pile of clothes, still holding me tight against him. Once more that mighty maw opens, and I scream as the monster charges us. Lo'zar sweeps up his gun, spins around, and fires.

BANG! The shot is deafening. The bullet meets the creature's head, splattering us with blood. It slows, legs crumpling underneath it, and falls to the ground in front of us in one big heap.

I'm panting as Lo'zar lowers the gun. That's when I realize we're pressed against each other, naked and breathing hard. Water drips down Lo'zar's sculpted chest, running in rivulets all the way to his groin. My nipples are puckered from the cold air and the feel of his skin on mine. I try not to look down, but I can't help myself.

His cock is even bigger now, thick and full and darker than the rest of his skin, with big veins branching their way up the shaft. Just looking at it, seeing how full with need it is, sends a sudden shock down into my hips. I can feel the entire length of it against my belly.

Quickly Lo'zar steps back and covers himself, trying to push it down with one arm the way someone might wrangle an unruly pet. He laughs awkwardly, and I remember that I, too, am standing there with my breasts exposed for the whole world to see. I turn away and cover myself with my tied arms. As he puts his pants back on, Lo'zar's face turns a deep purple.

"*Ag yazik,* Ree-mee?" he asks me, tilting his head. I think he's concerned about me.

I gape at him, then at the beast he just felled. "I'm okay," I answer. I dust off my arms like this was nothing. "Just fine."

With a charismatic smile, Lo'zar nods in approval. Then he notes the blood now covering both of us.

Time to wash off again.

When he leads me back to the cage I'm still completely naked. Once I'm behind bars, Lo'zar tosses me his long tunic, and I think he wants me to put it on. I slide it over my arms and find it carries the same warm, homey smell as the blankets. This must be Lo'zar's smell, the odd trollkin who saved my life.

I think then that I like it.

LO'ZAR

Well, damn. That was embarrassing.

I curse at my cock again for being so lewd at exactly the wrong moment. I don't need this little human to be any more afraid of me than she already is. But she didn't recoil, like I expected. In fact, she seemed fascinated by it, and that only turned me on more.

Now she's sitting inside her cage, as clean as I could get her without soap and dressed in my long shirt. I have an extra just so I'm not wearing the same thing for days on end, but Drozeg gives me a funny look when I slip the spare on over my bare chest.

"Enjoy your bath?" Kugara asks with a little flint in her eyes. "I heard a gunshot."

"It was kind of a pain." I wave a hand dismissively. "I had to off a hippo."

She looks satisfied by this answer. "Now that you're all done, we'd better get going. Our buyer is expecting us."

I take up my position in the back of the wagon near Ree-mee's cage as we return to the road and start moving again. The tiny human huddles inside my clothes, practically swimming in fabric, her wet hair dripping down the front where it softens the cloth and makes it stick to her nipples. Help me, it's practically see-through. Though she doesn't look up, there's a smile lingering on her face. I'm glad I could put it there when she has so little else.

We continue on in silence, which quickly grows dreary and boring. I twiddle my thumbs. I find a spare edge of twine and twirl it in my fingers, tying it and then untying it again. I tap the empty crate with a fist in a regular rhythm, remembering the drums that the older trolls often played around the fire pit when I was young. Anything to fill the endless time. I know that my impatience is one of my less redeeming qualities, but I can't help feeling restless while we draw closer and closer to the end.

Everything about this feels ugly and wrong.

Suddenly, something nudges my wrist. It's Ree-mee, crouched at the front of her cage, the collar of my tunic swooping low over her chest. I can see straight down it, right through her cleavage, so I quickly bring my eyes back to her inquisitive face.

She taps her finger once on a crate, then twice. Afterwards she falls still and waits, watching me intently.

Not sure what she's expecting, I decide to imitate her tap. Once, then twice, then nothing. A smile lifts the sides of her small mouth. I satisfied her, whatever it was she was after.

She taps again—four times. *Pa-pum, pa-pum.* It reminds me of the sound of a heartbeat. So I tap the same number of times, in the same rhythm, and her smile brightens.

Once again, she taps the first series of sounds, and I mimic her. Then the second. Soon we're tapping together in a regular rhythm. Ree-mee nods in satisfaction, pleased with my performance. I have no idea what I'm doing, but I guess I'm doing it well.

Now that I'm going with the beat, she changes her own tapping. She hits at half-notes, and moves her hand to a different part of the crate, making a new sound. Her tapping adds exciting flavor to whatever song we're making, and once again I'm reminded of the older trolls playing drums, jamming to some tune that the rest of us couldn't hear. She taps her other hand on the bars of her cage, adding a surprising metallic ring to the little band. So I bring in my own second hand, and once we have a rhythm going between us, I start riffing. I'm using all four fingers to make a fast-paced beat, my rings jangling when they collide, and now Ree-mee is grinning. All I want to do is keep making her smile like that.

"Stop making a racket back there," Kugara calls from the front of the wagon. My hands still. Ree-mee looks up, and then back at me with a questioning look in her eyes.

I make a harsh cutting gesture across my throat. The smile drops from her face.

No more percussion band.

Silence falls again, and it's ominous in the same way that arriving at our destination tomorrow feels ominous. Now that our fun game has ended, my gut is dreading it. What's going to happen to her there? What will they do to her when she inevitably fights back?

I twist my rings around my fingers absently, trying not to imagine it in detail. I've acquired them one at a time since I joined the clan, to keep my coin close to me in a way that no one can steal it—unless they cut off my hands, of course. Rimi follows the motion with her eyes, cocking her head curiously as she studies them. I splay my fingers so she can get a better look, and a shy smile tilts up her mouth as the jewels reflect the light back at her.

Suddenly, I want to know everything about her, this strange human woman who feels music, who has such a sweet smile. Who is tiny Ree-mee? How did she get here? Where is she from?

I can't ask her these questions, though, so I try to make up answers just by looking in her eyes. They're bright gray, like a storm cloud, and I can't help feeling like she's foreign. Strange. Not just because she's a human in trollkin lands, but because she's otherworldly. Even in the human capital, she wouldn't belong.

I wonder if she's from far away, and that's why she feared the crate so much. Did they ship her a long distance in one? I wish there was some way I could talk with her.

What would I say if I could?

RIMI

I think Lo'zar might be my only way out of here.

For some reason, he's different than the others. He's done his best to make me comfortable and fed. He could've taken advantage of me at the river, but he didn't.

I keep wondering if he has some ulterior motive, some reason for treating me with kindness, when the other trollkin only see me as an animal. Perhaps he likes me, just enough to play a tap battle with me and decide it was worth stopping to bathe me.

The idea of escaping had never crossed my mind before because it had seemed utterly impossible. But out here in the wilderness, surrounded by jungle... My chance is calling to me. If I'm ever going to get out of this, the time would be right now, before we reach wherever we're headed.

Lo'zar is the keystone. I need to convince him to free me.

I'm pretty sure the three trollkin are all mercenaries of some kind. Hired help, which could mean their loyalty doesn't run too deep. And he definitely desires me. He'd been more than erect during our bathing excursion, and I couldn't help the twinge of satisfaction I got from knowing I'd caused it. He is strangely attractive, I have to give him that—a whole wall of sleek muscle and thick arms. He tries to hide his interest with his cocky smile, but it's there underneath.

And if that hard dick of his was any indication, there might even be more. An inkling of lust that maybe I can use for my own purposes.

That night when Lo'zar passes off some of his rations to me, I let my fingers linger on his just a moment longer than necessary. The hair on my arms rises at the skin contact. The first time I do it, his eyes jump up to mine, and there's a curious look in them.

The second time I do it, they are less curious and more perplexed. The third time, he gets a knowing smile, and he arches an eyebrow at me dramatically. Shit—he knows what I'm trying to do. He says something I can't understand, then laughs to himself, and passes me another piece of meat. This time, he takes all of my fingers between two of his, and gently tugs my hand towards him.

Then, looking me right in the eyes, he says, "Ree-mee *kagez gizak, ganarr?*"

I wish I could understand him. I just furrow my brow, and he sighs. Then he drops my fingers and passes me another piece of meat. He doesn't take my hand again, but I can tell that he's paying closer attention to me now, studying me. I wish I knew what he was thinking. I wish I could beg him to let me free.

CHAPTER 5

LO'ZAR

I saw right away that she was trying to butter me up so I'd help her get out of there. But there's a good reason I've never been caught working in this business as long as I have: I'm good at sniffing it out when something's a little fishy.

Yet it does make me admire Ree-mee even more, knowing that she's shrewd. She wants to escape, and I'm part of her scheme.

I try to tell her that she doesn't need to offer herself to me in exchange for getting out of here. If I could speak her language, I'd say that I've already been formulating a plan after Kugara killed our jam session.

There are a few options, if I actually want to do this, which I'm still not sure that I do. I know that I can't simply watch her get beaten or raped by whoever purchased her and ordered her shipped here. But that means defying Gusak, which would inevitably lead to getting my limbs cut off one at a time until I bleed to death—if I'm caught. Not my favorite way to go out.

If I'm not caught... that means I can't ever go back. I would be dead to the clan, the place where Graz and I finally made our home after sleeping in dark corners our whole lives, where my skill in staying hidden, in taking what I need without being seen, is valuable to someone. I earned coin and recognition instead of being kicked and hollered at.

If I do this, I'll always be on the run from Gusak.

Anyway. Back to the escape plan.

Option one is to get up in the middle of the night, open her cage, and then go back to bed and pretend I didn't hear or see anything. If I could put down the right clues, I could make it look like she got herself out and take at least some of the heat off of me.

But there are downsides, the main one being that I would be freeing her from captivity, where she has meals and shelter, and abandoning her in the jungle to be killed by jaguars or hippos.

Option two is to get up in the middle of the night and sneak off with the wagon and the horses while Kugara and Drozeg are still sleeping, leaving them stranded in the jungle until they can get back to Kalishagg and tell Gusak what I've done.

Hopefully by then I'll be far away.

But this is not the sort of thing you do lightly. Am I really going to give everything up for some human?

Probably.

She doesn't deserve this, whatever happened to bring her into my possession, and I have a *responsibility* to keep her safe. It comes over me abruptly, the way a young troll gets his first crush and realizes what his cock is for. A deep kind of knowing, where no matter how hard you try, you can't resist its pull. Not only do her gray eyes speak to me, they *see* me. Her quick little mind deserves freedom.

Not to mention she's absolutely beautiful, like the first flower emerging from the ground after a long winter. Flowers should not be cut and left to rot in cages.

I know what I have to do. It's dangerous, but I have no choice.

Maybe there's a reason that I ended up assigned to this job: because Ree-mee needs me.

We only have a day left until we reach the buyer, maybe less by the glance I'd gotten of the map. That means arriving tomorrow afternoon. If I'm going to do it, it'll have to be tonight while the others are asleep.

We stop for the night a little after sunset, while the sky is still a warm purple, and find a place by the side of the road to make camp. Kugara builds a fire, and I stalk out into the woods to see if I can find a creature to hunt for dinner. We always have rations, but tonight I want to cook up something fresh and delicious, something that will make the other two sleep heavily and soundly.

After a while, I manage to spot one of the tiny little deer that call the jungle home, no bigger than a dog, but stuffed with plenty of warm meat for the four of us. It's not hard to bring it down with my gun—just one bullet to the head—and then I carry it back to camp over one shoulder.

"Nice," Kugara says, nodding in approval. "Dinner is served."

Ree-mee is pleased with the cooked meat I give her, and this time, the brush of her hand across mine feels different. Affectionate. Grateful. She smiles again, showing off all of her perfect white teeth, and my heartbeat quickens.

It doesn't slow down as night falls and we spread out our bedrolls around the fire. In fact, it's beating so hard and so fast as I consider my plan that I wonder if the others can hear it, if the rapid thumping of it will give me away.

Once a few hours have passed and I'm certain Drozeg and Kugara are in their deepest sleep, I get up and make my way over to the wagon. I'll need Ree-mee to be completely silent for this to work. That's my biggest gamble.

In the dim light of the moon, I can make out her sleeping form in the back of the cage. Gently, quietly, I reach out and tug on her blanket. Her eyes flutter open, and she looks confused as she glances around to find it dark outside. Then her gaze lands on me and her lips part. I can't help thinking that they look extremely kissable.

I put one finger to my mouth and shake my head, hoping she'll understand that I don't want her to make a sound. Her eyes widen, and when I reach for the bolt that latches the cage shut, her lips tilt up on one side. I slide it open as quietly as possible, and then gesture for her to come out with one hand.

Cautiously, as if she doesn't believe that I'm really going to help her, she reaches out and takes my fingers in hers. Then she steps out of the cage, using me to stabilize herself, and for a second I wonder if she's going to take off on her own. I remember from transferring her to the cage that her flight response is strong, even if she doesn't have much strength left from all her time in captivity.

I help her down from the wagon and set her on the ground. She weighs almost nothing. Ree-mee looks out towards the jungle, and she tenses as if to run. My biggest gamble was that she would be greeted with her freedom and decide that I'm still her enemy.

But then she looks back at me, an inquiring look in her eyes. I point at the ground and hold up a hand, trying to tell her to stay put for now.

The first thing I do is pack a bag of supplies and leave it by the fire. When I steal the horses and wagon, I'll be stranding Kugara and Drozeg out here. The least I can do is make sure they have enough food and water to walk home. Then I clean up my bedroll and pack it in the wagon, trying to keep as quiet as I can. Kugara shifts in her bed and lets out a snort, and I freeze. If she wakes up now, I'll definitely be fucked.

But she just rolls over onto her other side and snores. With a breath of relief, I retreat back to the wagon, where Ree-mee is patiently waiting for me. I'm grateful she trusted me enough to not wander off on her own. She must sense that I have a plan.

One of the horses huffs as I re-attach them to the front of the wagon. It makes some noise as I hook up their leather straps, and each time the wood creaks I pause to glance back at Drozeg and Kugara. As I'd hoped, they're sleeping hard.

Once the horses are ready to go, I gesture for Ree-mee to follow me, and then I lift her up into the front of the wagon. When I climb in next to her she scoots over to make room, and I can't help but smile. Tentatively, she smiles in return, and I shake the reins.

This is the moment, of course, that I hear Kugara's sharp voice say, "What are you doing, Lo'zar?"

I glance back at the encampment, where she's abandoned her bedroll and is now scrambling for her hand axe. But it's too late. I rap the reins harder and let out a whistle, no longer afraid of waking up the others. The horses jump from a walk into a trot. But Kugara is fast, and she's already sprinting towards us at full speed.

"Hup!" I call out, shaking the reins even more vigorously. "Hup!"

We burst into a gallop just as Kugara reaches out for the rear gate of the wagon. She reels her arm back and hurls the axe—and I duck just in time to avoid being beheaded.

"Lo'zar!" Kugara shouts after me. "Gusak is going to kill you for this!"

And he probably will, if he can get his hands on me. But if there's anything in life I can say I'm good at, it's swiping the treasure and getting away with my hide intact.

I can't help but holler back, "Let's see him try!"

CHAPTER 6

When he let me out of the cage, I thought about running. It could have been my chance to be free, perhaps even to find my way back home.

But when he told me to stay, I thought of the big brown creature that came out of the water. There are many unknown dangers out in the jungle, but Lo'zar? He seems to have a plan, and after what I've seen him do so far, I want to know what that plan is. Besides, now that it's only the two of us, it'll be easier to run if I need to. I could simply whack him over the head with a pan and take off into the jungle if things turn south.

Lo'zar pushes the horses hard for the first few miles, and small objects fall off the wagon as we bump and bang along the uneven road. But he doesn't stop to retrieve them, so I hold on and try not to bounce right out.

I wonder if he's just running off with the loot. Or maybe he plans to deliver me to my destination alone and take the money—and the credit—for himself.

Yet I can sense that's not true. His sharp eyes are focused on the road ahead, his mouth in a tight line and his tusks drawn high up on his face as he concentrates on making our escape. He'd been brash as we ran off with the wagon, but now his tense shoulders belie a deeper fear. Whoever we left behind, I have a feeling it's not the last we'll see of them.

So why would he risk all this? It can't be... for me?

Even if I'm just a casualty in his heist, at least I'm no longer in a cage. I wish I could convey to him the bright light of hope he's kindled in me. But I can't, so I stay quiet, trying not to distract from the uneven road ahead of us.

I don't realize that I've started to drift off to sleep until my head lands on something soft. I jerk and sit up to find that I've been leaning on Lo'zar's big arm. He glances down at me, and a mischievous grin plays across his face. Lifting up his arm, he gestures at me to get closer.

I frown. What is he going to do? So far, though, he hasn't tried anything untoward, so I scoot towards him on the bench and his arm drapes over my shoulders. He pulls me against his side, then tilts my head so it's leaned on his chest. He says something in his language, something soft and sweet, and I think he's telling me to go to sleep.

Not all trollkin are monsters, I decide then. There is something good in this one, even if I don't understand it yet, even if he can't tell me what we're running towards—or away from.

As the sun starts to rise in the distance, bathing the jungle in soft orange, my eyes fall closed and I drift off with Lo'zar's arm wrapped around me.

I'm not sure how long I've been asleep when the wagon comes to a halt. It's daylight now, and it warms my skin wonderfully. Combined with Lo'zar's comforting smell, I'm loath to wake up.

Then voices echo off in the distance. Lo'zar jumps out of the wagon with fear on his face, then picks me up and tosses me into the back like I'm a sack of goods. He grabs a cloth, handing it to me, and mimes covering himself with it. So I do as I'm told, lying down in the back of the wagon and drawing the cloth up over my body. My shoulders are shaking, hoping that I'm not seen. If we were discovered now, everything Lo'zar's risked so far would be for nothing.

The wagon rocks when he hops back into the driver's seat and we continue at a walking pace. There comes the sound of hoof-beats. Lo'zar says a greeting, and unfamiliar voices return it. Then we continue on, and relief washes over me when no one comes to tear the cloth off of me. We did it.

After a while Lo'zar calls out, "Ree-mee, *ag kagaz*." I don't know what it means, but he did say my name, so I poke my head out of the cloth. He's grinning as he pats the seat next to him.

This is our new routine as the wagon continues on down the road. Anytime we hear other people coming, I jump into the back and carefully disguise myself as part of the cargo. But after a while, I notice Lo'zar's eyelids are drifting farther and farther down. Driving the horses all night and day is catching up to him. When his head suddenly lolls forward, I reach out and grab his shoulder, taking the reins before they can fall and jerking them back. The horses neigh, confused by my rough hand.

His head jerks up and he looks around with confusion. I wave my hands in front of his face, giving him a concerned frown. He needs rest, I realize. So I mime sleeping, just resting my head on my hands, and then point at him.

But Lo'zar doesn't look too sure. He glances behind us, as if expecting the other two trollkin to appear at any moment, even though we've long left them behind. I shake my head, *no*, and make the sleeping gesture again. We both need some real rest. Surely there's no way the others will catch up to us on foot. Finally, Lo'zar acquiesces, and we pull as far off the road as we can without getting the wagon stuck in the dense foliage. First he hobbles the horses, spreading grain on the ground, then he unrolls a bedroll on the jungle floor. He sits back, rubbing his chin as if noticing for the first time there's two of us and only one bed.

That's when he gestures at me to get into it. The one bedroll, for me? I shake my head, but he's insistent. He lies down on the hard ground next to the bedroll, then stretches and yawns contentedly, as if to assure me that he doesn't mind it.

I can't help but smile at this strange creature who has decided to be kind to me. I never expected chivalry from a trollkin.

Sun drifts through the impossibly thick foliage overhead, dappling his face with little bright spots of light. His eyes close and almost immediately, his breath evens out.

What's going through his mind? I study him in the light, and it reminds me of an oil painting that would be hanging in our home. I wish I knew where we were going, or who we're running from. But I have no way to ask him, so I settle down into the soft bedroll that smells like Lo'zar and quickly follow him into sleep.

LO'ZAR

When I wake up, it's dark, and I panic for a moment that we haven't gotten far enough—that Kugara and Drozeg are just about to catch up to us. My panic rears up even higher when I find that the bedroll next to me is empty.

Where did she go? Blood rushes to my head when I jump to my feet, and I frantically search the jungle around us for any sign of little Ree-mee. Surely she wouldn't be so foolish as to leave on her own, would she?

"Lo'zar?" I hear her small, inquisitive voice over my shoulder and turn around to find her hopping down from the wagon, carrying a big bag. The moonlight turns her hair and face silver, like her eyes. She jogs over to me, and plops the bag down on the ground.

"Ree-mee," I reply, and reach out to touch her shoulder, as if I need to make sure she's real. She lets me do it, and I exhale with relief. "You're okay." She cocks her head, confused by my tone. I pat her a few times to reassure myself that she's still here.

She rummages through the bag. I realize when she's pulled out a few fabric items that this must be Kugara's stuff. Ree-mee extracts a pair of stitched pants, and though Kugara is significantly taller and wider, they should fit her well enough with the laces drawn tight. I'd almost forgotten she's still only wearing my extra-large tunic because it covered her like a dress. She slips on the pants, and then pulls out a few shirts, examining each like she's on a shopping spree through Kugara's clothes. Once she's found what she's after, Ree-mee turns around and takes off my oversized shirt. Her back is creamy smooth, and just the sight of her small shoulders and the generous curve of her hips immediately makes me hard. Damn.

I'm hungry for her, I realize. This strange human with the sharp mind and tapping fingers has left me starving. But I stay where I am, and squeeze my hand into a fist to keep it still.

Ree-mee slips on Kugara's much more appropriately-sized jerkin—still much too big for her tiny human frame—and turns back around, smiling widely. I study her for a moment, then give a nod of approval. She lifts the hem of the shirt and curtsies, and it's so damn cute that my cock surges against the inside of my pants.

Now that we're both awake, it's time to go. It'll be at least two days until Kugara and Drozeg make it back to the city and tell old

Gusak what happened. Once he knows, though, all bets are off. He'll send riders out as soon as possible, *fast* ones, and then we'll have a huge target painted on our backs.

We have to put as much distance as possible between us and Kalishagg while we still can, and at some point, diverge from the main path to make it harder for them to follow us. We have to get out of the jungle, at the very least. It's not safe for her or for me.

After we've eaten and had some water, I lift Ree-mee into the wagon and we're on our way, our path lit by the glowing moon. I still don't know where we're going—I probably should have figured that out—but we'd better move quickly.

Now that I've freed her, perhaps my next step is to get her to safety, and the only place she'll be truly safe is within the human lands. But we're a long way from any human settlements out here. We'd have to make it to another port city, Borzan, and then take a boat across the bay, which would land us near some contested territory. From there, we'd have to find another method of travel until we reached human civilization, and only then would Ree-mee really be safe.

Our other option is to continue walking and go the long way around. It would take us through the hills, where bandits are known to seize travelers, steal their goods, and usually murder them.

I would really prefer the not-murder route, myself, but smuggling a human into Borzan and then onto a boat without getting caught—either by the guards or by Gusak's men—sounds like an impossible task.

And that's if I just wanted to take her to a human settlement. The other option, the one I only barely consider before setting it aside, is to get her back to her home to where she belongs. But where that is... I don't know if I'll ever find out.

Then I'd have to think of myself, of where I can possibly go now that Gusak's hounds are after me. Who knows how much he sold Rimi for? He'll be enraged.

Maybe I should have had a better plan before I ditched Kugara and Drozek in the jungle, but it's too late now. I've spent my life running missions for Gusak and cleaning up after him, overcoming impossible odds to stay ahead of lawmen. This is no different. Now Ree-mee's safety is my mission, my objective, and I won't rest until I finish it. I'll figure out the rest later.

It isn't long into the following day when I hear hoofbeats. Ree-mee jumps into the back of the wagon without having to be told, and covers herself up with the cloth. She's quick and smart, and my admiration for her only grows as she tucks herself into a pile of goods so you'd never know she was there.

The hoofbeats are fast. Galloping. A pang of dread hits me square in the belly, and I know better than to ignore my intuition. I pull the horses over to the side of the road and drop my hand to my gun. I only have a handful of bullets and powder on me, so if I must use one, it needs to count. Making sure the gun's packed and ready to fire, I pull out the map and pretend to be studying it as the hoof-beats approach.

Up ahead the road curves, so I can't see who's coming until they're almost on top of us. There are three of them, riding solo on their horses, and the moment I see the leopard furs over their shoulders and glowing purple eyes, I know that we're fucked.

Hunters.

"Ree-mee," I hiss. She pokes her head up under the cloth. I jerk my head to one side, leap off the wagon and run to the back. Then I pull the cloth off of her and yank her up by one hand. Shocked, she resists for a moment, so I seize her by the waist and haul her out of the wagon. By the time I've got her on the ground, kicking and flailing, the riders have almost reached us. I wish Ree-mee could understand me.

If I thought Gusak's riders were bad, they have nothing on wild trolls. For the most part, they keep to themselves and don't bother travelers. But their hunters are another story. Hunters are trained from an early age to find and kill, whether their target is animal or trollkin. There have always been urban legends that not only will they brutally murder you, they'll also cook and eat your meat before they're done with your corpse. Whether that's true or not, with eyes like those, I don't want to find out.

The riders roar something I can't understand. I pick up the little human and toss her over my shoulder, and take off into the trees as fast as possible.

I can't let anything happen to her.

Chapter 7

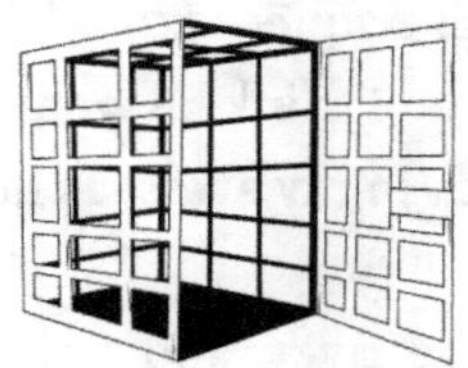

Rimi

I'm yelling as Lo'zar throws me over his shoulder like a bag of potatoes and charges off into the jungle. Why are we running? The three trollkin are shouting after us as he sprints, my legs flailing behind him. Are they the same people who were keeping me captive before?

No—I don't think so. By the way Lo'zar reacted, I think they might be something even worse.

Branches and leaves whip me across the face, so I cover myself with my hands while Lo'zar keeps me anchored by the waist. That's when I hear them behind us, stomping through the brush. Lo'zar takes an abrupt turn and speeds up, perhaps hoping we'll lose them. We crash through the trees, and I marvel at the trollkin's physical power as he leaps over a fallen log and lands on a boulder, taking another leap until we're on the ground again. His shoulder is digging into my stomach, making everything we ate earlier lurch and smash against my insides. But I've stopped fighting now that I understand he's trying to save us.

I hear our pursuers gaining, and Lo'zar does too because he takes another sharp turn, diving into a thick curtain of vines. Up ahead there's a river, and the closer it gets, the more I realize it's much too big for him to simply hop across. He slows for a second, grabbing both of my arms and then sliding me over behind his back, where he wraps my hands around his neck so I'm hanging on like a baby monkey. With a squeeze to my wrist, he says something in his language firmly, and I think he wants me to hold on tight. So I do, with all the strength in my arms, as he grabs onto a huge vine and jumps.

It swings us over the river, and I think that certainly we're going to fall right into the water. But when Lo'zar releases the vine we go flying, and he lands on the very edge of the far riverbank. Before I know what's happening, we're running again and I'm clinging to Lo'zar's neck with everything I have. Angry roaring fills the jungle. Somehow, my trollkin picks up his pace even more, leaning forward as we blow past trees and ferns. We're heading uphill, and Lo'zar's breaths become heavy and ragged as he hauls both of us along as fast as he can. I'm just a dead weight, I realize, holding him back.

Up ahead, I glimpse some stone through the trees. As we near, more and more of the structure becomes visible. It's some kind of ancient, crumbling ruin, with high walls that have collapsed over time. Trollkin used to live here, hundreds or thousands of years ago, but now their homes have been abandoned and overgrown by trees. Lo'zar bounds onto a pile of broken stone, then grabs a rough ledge above us and pulls himself up. How he's able to carry my weight and his, I have no idea, but he manages to climb over the the wall just as our pursuers appear through the trees—three huge blue trollkin, with long tusks like Lo'zar's, wearing leopard furs over their shoulders and armor made of what looks like bones. Their eyes are the most noticeable part of them, glowing with a purple madness. They're hollering wildly, and though I can't understand the words, I know what they mean.

Whoever they are, they're after our heads.

Soon the trees give way to sunlight. When we burst through, Lo'zar comes to a halt.

We're standing on a cliff, only a few paces away from the river where it cascades off the edge in a huge waterfall. The sound of the falls deafens me. I can't see down over the cliff, but I know that now, we've run to the end of our luck. There's nowhere left to go.

That is, until I hear Lo'zar say something to me in a soothing voice. "*Gurzak kagnik,* Ree-mee," he whispers. And I know that he's going to jump.

I let out a screech as he steps off the edge, and we plummet through nothing. Air whips past, throwing my hair up above us. I'm screaming as we fall, and it feels like we're falling forever. I'm holding onto Lo'zar with all my strength, my eyes tightly closed.

We're going to die. There's no way we're not going to die. At least it will be quick.

There's a huge splash, and frigid water envelops me. I'm trying to hang on but my hands and arms have grown weak, and the water slips between us, separating me from him. I scream Lo'zar's name but instead, water rushes into my mouth and lungs and I choke on it. I flail with arms and legs, hoping I can swim to the surface, but we're so far down I can't tell which way is up.

Suddenly arms wrap around me and Lo'zar is right there, worry etched into his face. He holds onto me tight with one arm as he swims, his powerful legs pushing the water down with such force I feel it ripple past me.

And then, we're on the surface. I suck in air, but I already have water in my lungs that's coming up in a horrid cough. Thankfully, Lo'zar is still holding onto me and I know he won't let me go. As he paddles along, keeping me nestled in one arm, I choke and gag.

Before long I can breathe again in fits and spurts, and I've never been so grateful.

Now I can look around us, and I get a glimpse of what looks like an island. What's more arresting than sight of land is what's on top of it: An immense pyramid, the point shooting high up into the sky. It's falling apart at the edges, but a surprising amount of it is still intact.

"Ree-mee *ag nak grozzak?*" Lo'zar asks, looking over at me. The water is just under his chin, and I can tell he's struggling to swim while also carrying me under one arm.

"I'm fine," I say between gasps. "Let me go. I can swim." I used to do laps in the lake every day in the summer to get away from the tension in the house as my parents argued about money. But Lo'zar can't understand me, so I peel his arm off and paddle onward.

"Ah," he says, and lets me go. He points ahead at the island. I want to say, *yes, of course*, but I follow along behind him as he heads towards it.

It only takes a few minutes for us to reach the shore, and once Lo'zar is out, he reaches down to help me up. When we're finally on dry land, I fall to my knees and cough, which pulls out the rest of the water that got inside me. Lo'zar pats my back, saying my name as he does.

He saved my life. Why? What does he have to gain? He could have left me behind when those trollkin with the furs came after us, but he slowed himself down to bring me along.

I catch him glancing over his shoulder, back at the cliff. Once I have I've regained my breath, he takes me by the elbow and urges me to my feet. Whoever they are, Lo'zar clearly thinks the monsters chasing after us are willing to follow us down here.

With a few stuttering steps I manage to get up to my feet, and Lo'zar takes off at a run. I keep up as best I can, but his legs are much longer than mine, and I fall behind as we reach the base of the huge pyramid. There are towering pillars everywhere, topped with massive carvings of trollkin heads. I wonder briefly who lived here, and what this pyramid was for. Is some ancient king or queen buried here, on this strange island surrounded by water and cliffs?

There don't appear to be any doors or entrances leading into the pyramid. Up ahead I can make out a staircase, carved with steps that scale the side. It must be hundreds of feet high, I think. He can't mean to climb them.

But when we finally reach the structure, Lo'zar starts up the stairs.

"Wait!" I call out, gasping. I lean forward, hands on my thighs, and suck in air. My lungs are burning. Besides, what do we have to gain at the top of the pyramid? We'll just be funneling ourselves into one place for those trollkin with the leopard furs to find us. But I can't ask, and Lo'zar seems insistent that we go.

There's no way I can make it to the top, not right now.

Understanding crosses his face. This time when he picks me up, he tucks me against his chest, wrapping my arms around his neck so he's reaching under my butt to heft me up onto his hips. Once my legs are wrapped around him, my face pressed to his collar and one of his strong arms holding me like a child, he jogs up the stairs.

I'm so grateful to be alive I could just cry. Now here Lo'zar is, helping me again for whatever reason I can't fathom.

Instead, I cling onto him and hope he knows what he's doing.

LO'ZAR

Yeah, it's probably stupid. If my hunch that there's more to this ruin than meets the eye is wrong, the hunters could simply corner us at the top. My ears pick up their shouts in the distance, so I'm pretty sure they'll come after us, even up here. This is their territory, not ours, after all.

But there's no way out of this great big bowl, either. The lake is surrounded on all sides by cliffs as sharp and steep as the one we leapt off. From what I could tell when we emerged from the water, there didn't appear to be a path up and out again.

If I learned anything on the street, it's that when you can't wriggle your way out of a bind, find a good place to hide until the worst has passed. I don't know what lies inside the pyramid, but at the very least, I can funnel our attackers into a small space and pick off the hunters one at a time while Ree-mee goes on ahead. With their hatchets they don't stand much of a chance against my gun, at least not at long range.

And at short range, I'm deadly with a sword.

Holding my little human close against my chest, I'm highly aware of her body and how her breasts are rubbing against me, her legs around my waist and her face nestled in my neck. If I weren't running at full speed up a flight of a thousand steps, I would be really turned on. Instead, I'm panting, my body already ragged from our sprint through the jungle and the following mad swim.

But Ree-mee swam well, and I'm proud of her. In addition to everything else, she can be brave and fierce. Unfortunately, she is small and weak like a child, too. It's up to me to protect her.

I don't think it was coincidence that Gusak assigned me to this job, and there's a greater reason I ended up her caretaker. After a lifetime spent taking, hurting and sometimes even killing, I've been given a different job now: to keep Ree-mee out of harm's way and help her to safety, wherever that might be. I'm sure of it.

I'm gasping by the time we reach the top of the stairs, where the slopes of the pyramid spread out around us. You could slide down one on your ass—and get the worst rug burn of your life— from the top to the bottom. It would probably be a fun ride.

Up here at the peak, there's only one notable feature: another short set of steps leading down into a dark tunnel in the stone. Immediately I'm repulsed by it. Who would step into a black abyss set inside a gigantic pyramid that's likely thousands of years old? Even if there aren't mummies or booby traps down there, we'll still have to contend with cobwebs and spiders.

I turn around and survey our surroundings, setting Ree-mee down. Three dots are moving through the water to the west. I suppose we don't have a choice. I nod toward the entrance to the pyramid and grab Ree-mee's hand. She looks down at our hands, then at me, as if disbelieving that I would ask her to descend into the darkness. I don't have anything with me that could light it up. We abandoned all our stuff when the hunters appeared. But what choice do we have?

Wait. I dig into one pocket. The little fire starter that I'd accidentally taken from Graz when we had some hash together the other night.

I look around for anything we could use, and there's a big dead vine growing between two rocks. I rip it out, then bring up the fire-starter and light the dry wood. It takes a while for it to catch, but eventually it does. I hold it out in front of us and the dim hallway lights up.

Ree-mee steps forward, then looks back at me. I nod ahead.

"Go. I'm right behind you."

RIMI

Lo'zar holds up the torch, and it casts an orange glow down the ominous-looking stairway. He urges me to go on, so I do, even though this all seems like a terrible idea. They could easily corner us down here, and we'd have no means of escape if they blocked the only tunnel out.

Despite that, Lo'zar hasn't given me a reason not to trust him. He's done nothing but keep me safe, so I give a faint nod and start down the steps. He follows close behind, and I'm reassured knowing he's here with me.

Once we've reached the bottom, the stone hall pivots and continues on straight ahead. The light of day is fading behind us, sending a shiver down my arms. There are carvings along the walls, but we're keeping a quick pace and I don't get a chance to stop and look at them.

We reach more stairs and pivot again, descending deeper into the pyramid. What would happen if there was a sudden earthquake? We would be buried inside here. For some reason that thought sits at the forefront of my mind as we continue downward. Now the only light comes from the torch, and the walls are too close, too tight around us. My breathing speeds up, and my heart beats faster. I can almost see the tiny holes in the crate, feel the wood pressing in from all sides.

As if he can sense my anxiety, Lo'zar touches my shoulder.

"*Yag iz kag,* Ree-mee?"

I nod quickly. "I'm okay. I think." I take a few deep breaths, and we continue on.

Suddenly the hall stops, splitting off in a three-way intersection. I glance to Lo'zar for instruction, but when I look over my shoulder, he seems just as baffled as I am.

That's when I notice something to the left—a tiny burst of white. I squint and head towards it. Lo'zar follows, the torch lighting the way, and I wonder how long it will last.

As we get closer, I realize that it's actually light up ahead of us. Real sunlight. I rush towards it, and the tunnel suddenly gives way to a cavernous room. Light streams down from holes left in the ceiling filled with moss, and it's enough to see by.

I glance back at Lo'zar and raise an eyebrow. What do we do now? But I don't think he knows the answer, either. He's studying the walls, and I track his gaze to find he's staring at the black markings painted all along them, faded with time. They look like humanoid figures, but strange and contorted, and I wonder if perhaps it's writing of some kind.

The longer I look at it, the more I get a tingling feeling at the base of my neck, like we've found something more than just an ancient ruin.

Lo'zar follows the writing across the room, where another hallway branches off and continues on. He shoots a look back at where we entered, and his ear twitches as he listens.

When no sounds come, I hope that we're going to finally sit down and rest. I really wouldn't mind it after the experience we just had. But Lo'zar gestures for me to follow him. His face isn't scared anymore so much as curious, even a little excited. I wonder what we've found that I don't understand.

He continues into the next hallway, lighting the torch again, and I walk after him, taking the edge of his shirt in my hand. We can't get separated. I won't be in the dark, all alone, ever again.

More and more, Lo'zar is becoming my rock. He's all I have in this horrendous world, and I can't let him go.

Chapter 8

Lo'zar

Ree-mee holds onto me as we descend deeper into the pyramid, and I feel a rush of pride. She trusts me to keep her safe, to make sure nothing bad happens to her.

How does this small human make me feel so many things?

Now that I've seen the room upstairs, I want to know what else lies down here. And the T-intersection gave me hope that perhaps we could throw the hunters off our trail once they reach the pyramid. Maybe we can lose them in here.

I make sure to build a mental map as we go. First there was the three-way stop, and then the big room with the sunlight and the strange writing. Then we took a right, and now we're headed down again. I have to be careful, and make sure that we turn around in time to get back to the top before the torch burns down.

In the meantime, I hope we can find somewhere dark to hide down here where the hunters won't find us.

We reach another intersection, this time a path branching off of the main one. I decide to continue straight, and Ree-mee follows dutifully behind me, trusting me to lead us. I don't know exactly where we're going, but I get the sense these hallways are designed to be confusing, as if this pyramid is hiding something precious, something that outsiders aren't meant to find. I keep my map in my head, looking for patterns, and hoping our trail is twisting enough our pursuers will have a hard time following it.

Soon we stumble into another room with sunlight coming in, but even less can make it this far through the moss and vines growing inside the channels. This encourages me. I think these sunlit rooms are a sign that we're going the right way.

When I study the writing again, something inside me responds to it. I feel the overwhelming need to go *down*. I turn around to see if perhaps Ree-mee said something, but she's looking up at me with her big grey eyes, waiting for me to decide what we do next.

Maybe it was just my intuition. Though consciously this all feels like a bad idea, I know to listen to my gut—it's gotten me out of a lot of tight spots before—so we continue on, even though the torch is getting lower. Could we really feel our way back if it ran out?

And then...

There's light, but it's a different kind of light. Up ahead, a purplish glow fills the tunnel. Ree-mee stops behind me, pulling on my shirt. She points at the light and shakes her head, her eyebrows drawn with concern at this new development. It is an eerie color, and certainly not natural.

But some light can't possibly hurt us. Besides, she doesn't need to be afraid while she's with me. I hold out my hand to her, palm up, and look at her small face. I take in her tiny nose, the way Kugara's tunic hangs loose off her wee body, then I give an encouraging smile. When her five-fingered hand falls into mine, I squeeze it tight.

"I won't let anything happen to you," I tell her in my quietest, softest voice. She stares into my eyes for a long time, giving me that same look she did the first time I saw her inside the cage, where it felt like she was seeing right into my soul.

I never realized how much I wanted someone to see me until this moment, now that she does.

As I turn back toward the light and start walking, Ree-mee follows me, her hand still tucked inside mine. The light grows brighter, until we reach a set of stairs leading down to the bottom.

Only a few steps in, I get a glimpse of what lies ahead of us.

It's a vast, sprawling stone room, and we're standing high up above it. Our path extends down and diverges, both sides continuing along the wall of the vaulted space to another set of stairs. At the bottom lies an immense, strangely-shaped rock, covered in glowing strands—which are emanating the purple light that drew us down here. It casts everything in a strange, bright glow, illuminating the mostly empty floor.

I decide to head to the right this time, and Ree-mee follows me. I extinguish the torch because the purple light is bright enough to see by, and then we can use it to leave again later. We make our way around the edge of the room to the next set of stairs and descend, drawing closer and closer to the stone. There are designs carved into the walls all around us, and again, they feel deeply familiar to me, though I can't make out their meaning. Some look like troll heads, others like human ones. There are hands meeting in the center on both sides of the room, almost like they're embracing the stone.

Ree-mee runs her hands along the carvings as we pass by them, and I wonder if she's feeling what I'm feeling—like we've stumbled across something strange and otherworldly, just like her.

As we near the bottom, I can finally make out where the light is coming from: worms.

There are glowing worms spread all across the surface of the stone, burrowing into it and emerging again in other places. When we get close, the light is almost blinding in the darkness.

Ree-mee surges ahead of me, running right up to the rock. I reach out to stop her, because we don't know what these worms are yet or what they do, but she already has one in her hand, squirming and wriggling. She has a bright, white smile on her face and she gestures at the worm with enthusiasm.

"Yes, I see it," I say placatingly. It creeps me out, and I don't like her touching it. I urge her to put the worm back, but she thinks I want to hold it, so she reaches out and presses it into my hand. My fingers wrap around hers, the worm tucked between them. She says something hurriedly in her language, but I can't make sense of it.

I wish I could understand you, I think, looking down into her small features. *Even for just a moment.* How much could I learn, how many mysteries could I solve, if I could talk to her?

What a strange thing, I hear a voice say as Ree-mee stares down at the worm, trying to get me to take it from her. *What is it?*

I must be imagining it. It almost sounds like... her.

It's gross, is what it is, I think.

Ree-mee's eyes jump to mine. Her brow furrows and she tilts her head. *Lo'zar?*

It's surely her voice. I know how it sounds by now, because every time she's used it, I've committed it to memory.

Ree-mee? I think. *Is that you?*

Her eyes widen. *I can hear you.*

In our hands, the worm has stopped wriggling. We both look down and find its little purple body has shriveled, and the bright glow inside is fading. In my surprise I let my fingers fall open, and the worm drops to the ground.

Oh no! Ree-mee reaches for it. *Shit. Is it dying?*

It's her. It's definitely her. And I can understand what she's saying.

But I think the worm is already dead. I squint, guiding my thoughts to the words I want to say. *It's gone, Ree-mee,* I tell her as she stoops down to pick it up. The glow winks out, and all that's left is a shrunken body.

She drops it to the floor again in disgust, but then stares up at me, and her eyes are huge with wonder. *That really is you.* Her voice is awed. *And you can understand what I'm saying. Right?*

It must be true, because she's coming across in my mind as clear as a starry sky.

Yes, I think, making sure to form the words clearly in my mind. *I can hear you, Ree-mee.*

She giggles. *It's Rimi.*

Rimi? I've had it wrong this whole time. She giggles again and nods.

That's it. Lo'zar.

I smile at the sound of her voice. I like it. I like it immensely.

But how is this possible? she asks. *We don't speak the same language.*

I glance down at the worms, who have retreated a little from us, casting a dark shadow.

I don't know, I say. *I think... I think this place might be sacred.* I remember the markings in the other rooms. I look up at the carvings on the walls of a trollkin and a human, each staring intently at the other.

Sacred? Like, religious? She follows my gaze around the great hall.

Maybe. I don't know. These are ancient troll ruins. I don't know much about them, to be honest. I'm distracted by the fact I'm actually hearing Rimi talk to me. I want to wrap myself up in her soft words, and then maybe wrap her up in my arms, too.

Ruins, she says, in the way that anyone can speak into someone else's mind. *Filled with... Glowing worms.*

I chuckle at this. It really is the most bizarre thing we could have found here, in the base of this ancient pyramid. If I weren't looking at it, I probably wouldn't believe it myself.

Worms that somehow are letting us talk to each other, I add. She smiles brightly.

I always wish I could understand what you're saying. A funny look comes over her face. *You talk a lot.*

I guffaw, and the sound surprises her. Then her smile widens. *Yeah*, I say. *Got a lot of shit for that as a whelp.*

You just have a lot of thoughts, she says. *But from what I can tell... they're nice thoughts.*

It's such a strange compliment, but it feels good coming from her.

Thank you. I like yours, too.

I realize we've just been standing there, staring into each other's eyes like idiots. We have to figure out our hunter problem —but all I want right now is to keep talking with Rimi. Though I haven't heard any signs of our tails yet, surely they'll find their way down here, unless the pyramid is an even greater labyrinth than I thought. There's no other way out of this place except up. And even if we got out unscathed, I'm not sure how we would ever climb that cliff face again.

So here we'll stay for now, until we come up with a better plan, or face the hunters ourselves. There are three of them and one of me, but I've gotten in enough scraps that I might stand a chance. When they do come, I'll be ready. In the meantime... I want to understand Rimi better, to know all the shining silver thoughts swirling around her head. So I gesture at the ground and sit.

What is this place? Rimi asks, sitting down next to me, surprisingly close. Her knee is slightly touching mine, and I wish there was even more of her touching me.

I shake my head. *All I know is these are troll ruins. We lived here ages and ages ago.* Then I remember Graz's map, and the red dots on them. One of those dots should be... right around here. Maybe he was on to something.

Rimi looks up at the faces on the walls, the human and the trollkin only inches apart from one another. *I've never seen anything like this. If these are troll ruins, why is there a picture of a human down here?*

I follow her eyes to the bizarre image. *I don't know. But they don't look like enemies, when humans and trollkin have been enemies for... forever.*

Rubbing her chin, Rimi tilts her head. *Maybe we weren't always.*

I try to imagine that, a time when our peoples didn't constantly try to kill one another and steal each other's land. It seems impossible, and yet we're looking right at some pretty compelling evidence to the contrary.

You know, Rimi says, *history is longer than we think. In my country, we have legends that go back to before the existence of humans and trollkin completely.*

I study her. *In your country?* I ask. Now I can finally get answers to all of the questions I've been puzzling over since she first came into my care. *What happened to you? How did you end up here?*

Rimi's face falls, the memory clearly a raw wound. *Well, I was sleeping when they came for me,* she begins. *They stole me from my bed and put me into a sack, then shoved me into a crate and, I think, put me on a ship. I don't know how long I was on that ship, but it felt like forever. Like two forevers.*

I remember how she reacted to the crate and guilt sweeps through me. I just want to hug her, and erase all the horror she's been through.

I'm so sorry, Rimi. I run my hand over her knee, and she doesn't flinch or pull back. *I'm sorry I was a part of this. My own boss, my own clan, is responsible for what happened to you.*

She gives me a wan smile. *Everything that's befallen me wasn't your fault. You freed me, Lo'zar.*

Again, my name in her voice sends shivers up my spine. I just want to reach around her and pull her close, the way I did when she fell asleep against my shoulder in the wagon. But I'm also embarrassed to be one of her kidnappers, horrified at myself for not setting her free the moment I laid eyes on her.

I couldn't let you get sold off like cattle, I tell her. *You're... You're a person. Even if you are human.*

'Even if I am human'? she asks, an edge to her voice.

Well, like I said, we're enemies. Our people have been killing each other for who knows how long.

She shrugs. *I never saw a trollkin before now.*

I furrow my brow at this. *Where are you from?*

Yusala.

Where's that?

Rimi contemplates for a few moments before answering. *Relative to here? I'm not sure.*

I shake my head. A place with only humans, and a name I've never heard before. *You're very far from home, Rimi.*

The look on her face is as if she expected to hear this. *Yeah. I imagine so.* She stares down at the ground, and tears well in her eyes.

It's okay. I reach out and wipe one from her cheek. She looks up in surprise. *We'll get you home.*

We... we will? She doesn't look like she believes me for a second.

Of course. I know this with a certainty now. I need to help Rimi get back to where she belongs, not just to make up for what I did—for what Gusak did—but because it's what's right. It's my duty. *You should be back at home in your bed,* I tell her.

Strangely, not only do the tears continue, but they're flowing harder down her face. She buckles forward and drops her head into her hands, weeping openly.

Rimi? What's wrong? I put an arm around her and instinctively pull her close.

I doubt you can get me home if it's as far as we think it is, she says, leaning into me. *But it's sweet that you want to try.*

I just hold her like that while she sniffles and wipes her face.

Eventually I say, *Maybe it's not that outrageous. Maybe we can figure out where Yusala is. If they brought you here, we can get you back.*

I don't see my own optimism reflected in her eyes. She's given up hope of returning home, just like I have. But I chose this for myself. She's surrendering.

I only want to get out of this alive, she says. *Then maybe we can figure that part out.*

Right. We are at the bottom of a pyramid, hoping hunters won't find us and kill us and then maybe eat us. But at this moment, I don't want to let her go.

Who are we running from? Rimi asks. *Who were those guys after us? They weren't the same two we left behind.*

They're hunters, I answer. *Wild trolls. You saw that glow in their eyes?* She nods. *They're mad. I don't know what causes it, but those hunters we saw are the worst of them.*

I think of those bright purple eyes, and my gaze is drawn to the worms tunneling their way through the stone at the center of the room.

They definitely wanted to kill us. Rimi tilts her head up at me. *Thank you for saving me. Twice now.*

I had no choice, I say. *I can't let anything happen to you.* I lean down and breathe in her hair. I like the scent of her—it's tangy and sweet, like one of those pieces of jeruba fruit. At my words, I feel her relax into my chest, and she brings up one hand to my collar. It feels so good and so intimate that my heart stops beating for a moment.

I want her to touch me even more. And that is, of course, when I start to get hard. It's not obvious at first under my tight breeches, but as Rimi strokes her hand up and down, it grows more and more prominent. I cough a little, trying to distract her, but it's too late.

Oh, is all she says when she notices the significant lump in my pants.

Sorry. It just... For some reason this, um, happens a lot around you. I turn my head, rubbing a hand down my face in humiliation.

It's okay, she says. *It's a nice compliment.*

She thinks it's a compliment? That she makes me get thick and warm and swollen for her?

But you're a human, I say. I don't know why I'm reminding her. I would much rather not argue with her about how much she appreciates my boner.

So? You're not unattractive. Rimi arches an eyebrow at me. *And clearly I'm not, either.*

Her forwardness doesn't surprise me. Even though we couldn't communicate before, I still feel that I know who she is.

Not bad at all, I agree. *I like looking at you. I mean... I tried not to, though, that other time.*

Her face turns red remembering our little bath in the river. *Right. You did try. I appreciate that.*

Suddenly, she yawns, and I'm pleased that she feels secure enough under my arm to be tired after we've been chased and almost murdered.

Do you want to sleep for a while? I ask her. *I'll keep watch for the hunters. We should hear them coming if they decide to pursue us down here.*

Please, she says, yawning again. *I'm so exhausted. Even though you were the one doing most of the hard work.*

I grin down at her, and flex my arm. *No problem. I'm a strong troll.*

You are. She starts to drift to one side.

You shouldn't sleep like that, I say, tightening my grip on her. *I've got you. All right?*

She gives me an inquisitive look. I gently pick her up by her hips and slide her over my thigh so she's in my lap. Rimi lets out a squeak as her butt slides across my cock, and I try to will it to go down. Then I slip an arm under her neck to hold her up.

Just lie back and go to sleep, I say, supporting her in my lap with her legs hanging off my thighs. Without question, she does as she's told, drifting into the space between my elbow and my chest. I pull her closer to make it more comfortable, and she turns her face into me as she relaxes.

Thank you, Lo'zar, she says, her voice fading already.

You're welcome, Rimi.

Then she falls asleep.

Chapter 9

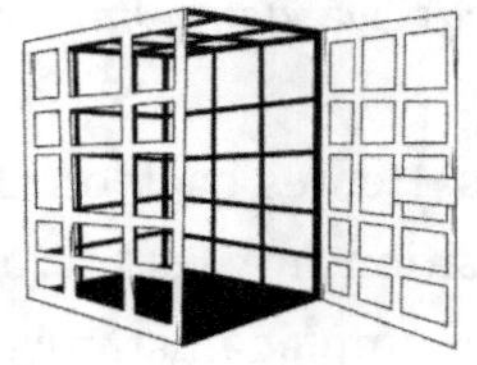

I can talk to him.

I can really talk to him. Finally.

Lo'zar is just as kind and gentle with his words as he is with his body. When he holds me close so I can sleep, I feel warm and safe knowing Lo'zar has his gun and his sword with him. The beat of his heart right next to my cheek is steady and sure, and I immediately drift away.

It's so cozy here that I'm reluctant to wake up again. When I open my eyes, Lo'zar is holding me while intently watching the tunnel where we entered. He takes his job very seriously.

Maybe you should sleep, too, I say to him, my voice jolting him out of his daze.

Lo'zar shakes his head. *They could still come. They're probably searching the whole pyramid for us.*

Hasn't it been hours now? I ask. He nods. *I think they gave up.*

Then we should leave, he responds. *Before they come back.*

I don't feel so certain that we should. Here, I can talk to him. If we leave, will we lose it? Will I never be able to hear him again?

Not that I have any idea how we'll get out of this valley, Lo'zar adds. *I didn't see any way up those cliffs we came down.*

That is a problem.

You should still get a little rest, I tell him. *Then we can figure out how to get out, now that we don't have those deranged monsters breathing down our necks.*

Lo'zar smiles at this. He lies back on the ground, still holding me against him, and positions my legs across his body so I'm using him like a bed. There's a lump against my thigh where he's getting a little thick under his pants. I imagine that big, purple-blue cock, which is now pressed up against me, and my skin feels warm everywhere Lo'zar and I are touching.

Sorry, he says, scratching the side of his nose in embarrassment. *You're just... hot.*

And I'm lying on top of you, I add.

He smiles at that. *Certainly doesn't help.*

But it's turning me on, too, feeling his hard chest under my hands, his cock nudging me. There's a warm seed of affection in my belly that's steadily sprouting into something else as I become aware of the way our bodies are rubbing against one another. I want more of it, in more places. Now that I can hear him talk, I feel like I can finally know all of him, and I want to have him skin-on-skin.

It seems like it's my turn to say something, to do something. Lo'zar would never touch me without asking, not unless I did it first. That's just the kind of guy he seems to be. So I reach out and take his bejeweled fingers in mine, and his eyes dart down to my face inquisitively.

What is it, Rimi? he asks. I know I should let him sleep, but I find that I want to go even deeper, to pursue this peculiar new feeling that's growing inside me.

I don't know, I confess. *I just wanted to hold your hand.* That's not all I'd like to put my hand on, but this feels safe for now.

That debonair grin of his reaches all the way to his eyes, pulling his tusks back. *Is that so?* He cups my fingers in his palm. *You're so small. I keep thinking that. How can anyone be so little?*

Perks of being human, I say. *And you're very big.*

I'm normal-size! For a troll.

I bat his arm playfully, and when I move, his insistent cock brushes against me again. There's a warm buzzing under my skin, and instantly I remember what it looked like, hard and swollen up in the river. Lo'zar sucks in a breath, and I think belatedly that I'm not being very kind by rubbing all over him, so I slide off until we're lying side-by-side on the stone floor of this great big room. He doesn't let go of my hand.

Sorry, I say.

He quirks an eyebrow. *For what?*

For, you know, getting all up on you.

A goofy smile tilts up his mouth. *I liked it.*

My heart does a little skip, and I return the smile. *I liked it, too.*

Lo'zar gently turns over so he's facing me, and raises his other hand to the side of my face. He traces a finger down from my brow to my chin. I want to look away because his gaze is so intense, but I find that I can't. I'm sucked into the feeling of knowing him. I can almost sense the size and shape and color of his soul. But I can't seem to hear all of his thoughts—and he only seems to hear mine if I'm not consciously hiding them. It's as if we share a special world that only belongs to us.

He leans towards me, closing the six-inch gap between our faces, his mouth just a hair's breadth away from mine and his tusks framing my face. I don't need to hear what he's thinking to know he wants to kiss me, so I brush the surface of his lips with my own, and in a split second his mouth is firmly on mine.

It's awkward at first with our different shapes, but he's insistent and passionate, bringing his hands up to my cheeks to draw me in closer. He opens my lips with his tongue, and I didn't expect just how good it would feel to kiss him, to taste him, or how much it would make other parts of me want his touch, too. Tentatively I open my mouth for him, and with a suave maneuver that is very Lo'zar, his tongue slips inside, seeking out mine. Soon they're playing together in the space between us and all it does is make me want more. I slide towards him along the hard stone floor until our bodies are pressed close together, and Lo'zar lets out a small groan into my mouth. He's stiff as stone against my thigh, and it makes me feel even more beautiful and wanted and warm with desire for him.

There was a boy when I was seventeen who I liked a good deal. He was a stablehand who came down to the lake after he was finished with his work for the day, and his was the first penis I really saw up close. We had gotten naked in a copse of trees far from the grounds, deciding to explore each other's bodies. But when it came time to do the deed he had pushed it inside me without very much warning. All I'd felt was discomfort, and an awkward throbbing feeling followed me between the legs for days afterwards. I didn't invite him to the lake with me again.

Would Lo'zar feel in my hand like the stablehand did? How would he feel inside me?

That last thought sends a shudder of anticipation down my spine. It's as if a bright string, vibrating with tension, now stretches between the place our mouths are touching and the warm core of my abdomen. Every movement of his tongue sends a ripple down it, until my hips are moving against his without my permission.

Rimi. Even Lo'zar's mental voice feels thick and heady. *Do you know what you're doing to me?*

The great thing about talking with your mind is you can keep kissing while you do it.

No, I don't, I say, nipping at his lower lip. He grunts and his hand drops behind my neck to pull my head even closer. *But I know what you're doing to me.*

And what's that? His hips respond to each sway of mine, rubbing his significant boner against the space between my legs.

Turning me on, of course.

Lo'zar chuckles into my mouth, pleased. *Oh, then we're in the same boat.* His hand travels from the nape of my neck to the small of my back. I marvel at the gentleness of his touch, this same troll who carried me over his shoulder through the jungle. But I can feel his urgency through it, too.

My desire is a flame, burning higher and brighter until it threatens to become a bonfire.

We've already seen each other naked, so a slow, tantalizing tease of removing clothes feels pointless. No, I want to see Lo'zar again like I did in the river, and this time I want to feel him, too. So I sit up and grab the hem of the tunic I stole out of the wagon, then pull it up over my head.

His eyes widen. *Oh.*

Do you want to stop? I ask. I don't know where we're headed yet, but I'm interested in embarking on the voyage anyway. As long as I'm with Lo'zar, I know nothing will happen that I don't want to happen.

A shocked look comes over him. *Please, don't stop. I want to see you. And then I want to touch you.*

Perfect, I say, abandoning the shirt on the floor. His eyes traverse me, wide and salivating. *I want that, too.*

Chapter 10

Lo'zar

Out of nowhere, my Rimi has started taking her clothes off for me. She's turned on by me. She wants me to look at her and touch her and—

I can't get ahead of myself. I have a golden opportunity here to finally experience her the way I've been wanting and I will not fuck it up.

When her shirt is off, I take in her round breasts with the generous pink-brown nipples, and my mouth waters. She's still sitting up on her knees and so I join her, crossing my legs in front of me. Tentatively, I reach out and run my hand over one pert globe, tickling the nipple with my palm until it hardens up into a bead. Then I repeat the motion with her other breast, and soon Rimi is gasping and twitching under my hands.

After I've sufficiently attended to her that way, I slide her towards me and heft her into my lap, where she lets out a sound of surprise at my cock insistently nudging her between the legs. But I ignore it for now, and descend on her nipples with my mouth.

Oh, Lo'zar. The soft sound of her voice echoes in my head as she moans underneath me. *That's so good.* I don't know if she intends to be saying these words to me or if she's just thinking them, but it's profoundly erotic either way. I want to make her sing even more like this. She's so responsive under my mouth, twitching and gasping as I nip and then soothe her nipples, that I could keep going forever. But there are more places I want to see, and things I want to do there to make her moan.

I pull away, and Rimi lets out a whine of disappointment. I reach down to take off my own tunic, and then holding her against me, lean forward to lay it on the stone floor. I lie her back on it and she goes without complaint, until she's flat and gleaming under the purple light.

These need to go, I tell her, tugging on the laces of her pants. The trousers are so big I could probably slide them off without trying, but I want her to do it. A wicked grin crosses her face, and I'm delighted by this sweet, clever, enticing human woman. She undoes the laces and I pull the pants off, revealing soft hips, thighs grown too thin from too little food, and a curly patch of hair between her legs. That's where I want to be. I want to drink her up and make her cry out my name.

I'm going to taste you, I say, sliding back so I'm crouching on my elbows above her hips.

There? she asks, eyes big. *Nobody's ever done that before.*

A tingle of thrill races down my back, straight to my cock. I'll be her first mouth ride. I can't wait.

I'll be gentle. And I will be, until she's slippery and crying out for more.

The stiffness fades from Rimi's shoulders and she takes in a deep breath as I crouch, placing my hands between her legs. I guide them apart, but I can tell she's reluctant to let me in, so I kiss from her knees, up her thighs and to her belly while my hand reaches down to her bundle of fur. When I find that soft place underneath with one finger, she's already warm to the touch, and her lower lips have swollen up. Good—she wants me, too. I gently cup her cunt in my palm, running my fingers up and down the outside of her.

Lo'zar, she thinks, her hips rising up to meet my hand. *How does that feel so good?* I'm barely touching her and she's already calling out for me.

Because I know what you want, I say, and it's true. It's as if I can feel her pleasure in my own body and my hands already know what to do. I bring my finger closer to the hidden button I know is waiting underneath her hood, and she jerks her hips, trying to draw me in to her most sensitive spot. But I won't let her have it, not yet. It's only once she's eager and moving in the same rhythm as my hand that I drop my head down and reach for her treasure with my tongue. When I lick her, she groans and arches her whole back, and I wonder how long it will take to make her come on my face. Probably not much for sensitive Rimi.

I relish the thought.

Flicking my tongue back and forth, I hold her thighs open while her muscles start to squeeze in. She's already close, I can tell. So I continue with my tongue, brushing over her sweet nub while she moans and writhes underneath me.

Lo'zar, her inner voice says feverishly. *I'm going to explode.*

I'm so glad I got to be the first one to taste her. *Let it happen,* I tell her. *Let it all go.*

I quicken my pace and continue tracing the outside of her small entrance with my fingers. No, I won't give her that, not just yet. She's already tensing up underneath me, her cute moans growing more urgent as I lap at her, occasionally stopping to suck her and twirl my tongue.

Oh, that's it. Her thoughts feel fragmented. *That's...*

Rimi's legs squeeze together and I let her do it, and she crushes my head between them. But I don't stop, even as she seizes and cries out, and soon she's thrashing and wriggling and reaching for my head with her curled hands.

I've never felt anything quite like that, her dizzy mind thinks.

As she starts to come down, my fingers seek out the slick hole I've only been teasing up until now. Gently I test her entrance, which is soaking wet for me, and Rimi instinctively pulls her hips back.

It's all right, I tell her. *It's going to feel good. I promise.*

As her body slackens, I test her tight cunt a second time until just the tip of my finger is able to slide in. She bucks and gasps. *Oh, wow*, she says. *That... that's amazing.*

Keeping my finger shallow I return to licking her, repeating the same motions that made her light up under me the first time. Soon she allows me in deeper, and then deeper, until I can start stroking the inside of her.

I know how to make a woman gush, and I'm going to make sure Rimi does as many times as I can.

Before long she's dripping into my hand, and in her head she's crying out her pleasure. *That's incredible, please*, she repeats, her tight sheath squeezing my one finger like a vice.

I wonder what she'll let me do. I slow down my hand and my tongue, so she has a moment to rest, before I start to explore with my second finger.

Lo'zar? she asks, a hint of concern in her voice as I start to wiggle it inside.

Breathe, I tell her. I've never been with anyone as small and tight as she is. But the second finger manages to fit, and she mewls as I gently move them both in and out of her. Once I'm licking her again, her mind becomes a jumble, sending me sounds and half-garbled words I can't make out. My mouth speeds up and so does my hand, and she's so wet that I'm slicking in and out without any effort. Her body responds to every stroke, and her cries are growing louder. I answer by moving faster and harder. I'm going to get her so ready for me that—

Wait. I don't even know if that's what she wants yet. She seems like a novice, and I don't want to scare her off.

Rimi is frantically swallowing up my fingers, and my shirt is all bunched up under her back as she bucks against me. I continue attacking her with my tongue until she's clutching my hair in one hand.

Lo'zar, I can't, she starts to say, and then it breaks off as she hits her wave and rides up and over the top. The scent of her orgasm hits me square in the nose this time, and I'm hopelessly hard and wet inside my own pants. My body only wants one thing, and that's to slide inside her perfect, soft cunt while she's still sensitive and tight.

I gently remove my fingers, and Rimi's hips fall back to the stone floor. She's panting hard, and her eyes are still closed.

What was that? she asks, wonder in her voice. *I've touched myself before, but it doesn't compare.*

I chuckle. *That's only a fraction of my power,* I tell her.

She sits up, staring at me with her mouth in a small circle. *There's more?*

There's so much more. I slide between her legs until I'm crouched over her, where I wipe off my lips with one wrist and lean down close. She kisses me, and she doesn't seem to mind the taste of herself.

Like what? Rimi asks. *Because if it's anything like that...*

Oh, it is. And better. My hand wanders down to her breast, rolling her nipple back and forth. It's like she's electrified under my hands the way she bends into me.

Then I want it, she says. *Show me everything.*

CHAPTER 11

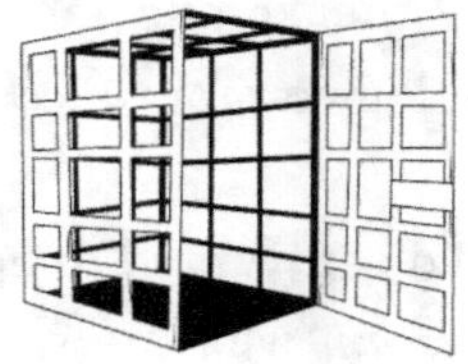

RIMI

Whatever it is that Lo'zar has to offer me, I'll accept it. I've never felt anything like this before, something that completely takes over and empties me of all other thoughts and feelings except *him*.

Lo'zar adjusts his shirt underneath me so none of my bare skin touches the floor, then rises up above me. He's enormous, I think belatedly. The biggest creature I've ever seen. He unties his breeches and then starts to pull them down—and that huge, swollen cock springs out.

I hadn't realized exactly how big it was, but now that it's right in front of me, I understand exactly what I'm dealing with. I know what he wants to do, and I'm almost certain that I want him to do it. The only part of me that hesitates is the part that lived in a cage, surrounded by monsters with terrible tusks who made me live in my own filth, who treated me like an object to be toyed with. They are, perhaps, even worse than the stories we were told as children.

But my troll is not one of those. No, he is kind and gentle. He's the one I want more than anything else.

Only if you're ready, Rimi, Lo'zar says, tossing aside his pants and kneeling between my legs. That massive cock is pointed right at me, a droplet of pale liquid running down from a slit right in the crown. I have no idea how such a thing could fit inside me, or if it would feel good. Even the stablehand's penis made me feel nothing but awkward and uncomfortable.

But it's so big, I say.

This clearly is what Lo'zar wanted to hear. He beams at me. *All the better to make you scream with,* he says, quite roguishly, and there's an aching feeling in my throat at the sight of his arched eyebrow and sideways smile. How is he so many good things all at once?

I know then that no one else in the world could please me the way Lo'zar can.

Okay, I say tentatively. *You'd better not be lying.*

I would never lie to you. And the way he says it, while looking me right in my eyes, assures me that he's sincere. *Have you ever gotten under the blankets with someone before?*

My face must go bright red, because Lo'zar chuckles. *Once,* I say, my shoulders curling. By now it probably should be more, but my parents have always kept me close to home, where I was to wait for a suitor to whom they could finally marry me off.

Lo'zar nods sagely. *It won't hurt,* he says. *But it might feel funny at first.*

I can handle 'funny.' *Then please,* I tell him, and with a deep breath, I spread my legs apart, exposing all of myself. Lo'zar's thick cock jumps at the sight of me. It's blue-purple, like his skin but darker, and a great big sac hangs below it. His gaze travels down my body and then up again, and he looks almost like he doesn't believe what he's seeing, either.

You're so gorgeous, Lo'zar says, then seems to remember what he was doing there. He lifts my hips up and then slowly guides himself towards the hot, wet place between my thighs. I wish I could see what it looks like as he brings the soft tip to the slit there, where I'm still dripping from his attentions. I feel it push me apart, reaching into the place where his fingers were only moments before. Suddenly I want nothing else than to bring it inside me, to feel all of Lo'zar and finally be as close to him as I've been hungering for.

But this object prodding at me is significantly larger than a few fingers. He leans forward and brings a hand up to my hair, pushing it gently behind my ear. His mouth drops to mine, and his tongue finds its way inside my mouth, just as he pushes inside me.

I gasp and flinch as my skin pinches. He's pulling me as wide as my body can possibly go, and it's only thanks to how slippery he's made me that he's able to get anywhere at all. I grip his shoulders hard and close my eyes, and I hear Lo'zar's voice in my head say, *It will pass.* And I believe him, because I know he would never lie.

He pauses where he is, letting my body adjust to him, and kisses me hard as if to distract me. That thick cockhead continues to ply me, in and out, taunting and tantalizing me with what's to come.

Soon, my muscles do start to relax, and he slides inside. I gasp and roll my hips as the feel of him overtakes me.

There we are, Lo'zar says, petting my hair, rubbing the tip of his nose over mine. His orange eyes are staring into me as he presses in deeper, and I stretch even wider to accommodate him.

"Oh!" All my muscles are flexing, consumed with the feeling of opening up to him. Somehow his cock gets thicker the deeper it gets, but still my body is drawing him in.

Suddenly, Lo'zar pauses, and he takes a few deep, calming breaths. *Rimi. You feel better than anything in the world.* He's panting. *I almost went off like one of Graz's fireworks.*

I stroke one of his tusks where he's hovered over me, imitating what I want him to do inside of me. *I'm glad you didn't. I want more of you.*

A wolfish grin spreads across his face. *More?* he asks, and then slides the rest of the way in.

I moan against him as his cock finds its resting place inside me. I've never felt this kind of fullness, this completeness, and it's intoxicating. I think that I could feel this way forever, our bodies joined in this most exquisite fashion.

But there's more. He slowly withdraws again, not quite leaving me but emptying me, and I let out a sound of protest until his head slips back in. I can feel every inch of him, and soon he's filling me up to the brim. My legs have found their way around his hips and all I want to do is keep him there, right where he belongs.

Lo'zar, I think, my pleasure breaking up my thoughts. *How do you feel so good?*

Because this is where I'm supposed to be, he says. And as another thrust fills me to bursting, I think that he's right. He must be right, because nothing has ever felt as pure and good as this, his arms wrapped tight around me as he takes me. When home is so far away, it's like I've found a piece of it here, with Lo'zar. I have a sense of belonging, when everything has been so alien and cruel until now.

Sparks are gathering in my abdomen, buzzing and swirling and spreading outward. He starts to thrust faster, kissing me hard, nibbling my lips and then swirling his tongue around mine. Each of his strokes shoots off a white-hot burst, and I find I'm moaning into Lo'zar's mouth.

Yes, he thinks. *You're amazing, Rimi.* I clutch him around the neck and he buries his face in my hair as he tests out every inch of me, listening to my responses and changing his pace or his angle with each stroke. How many times has he done this before? It must be a lot.

The sparks are growing as Lo'zar grunts into my ear, his arms pulling me even closer to him than I ever thought possible, and then—it strikes me like a bolt of lightning. I'm tightening up everywhere, each of my muscles straining to hold in this unbearable, explosive energy. I'm moaning his name, over and over, as he picks up his pace. I don't know how much more I'll be able to take before my whole body combusts.

Oh Lo'zar, I think. *I feel... I feel like... It's so...* All my words are mushing together.

I know. He strokes my hair as he thrusts all the way to the core of my being and out again. *Let me feel you.*

Lo'zar kisses my face, then my ear, panting against me. He's so dedicated to pleasuring me. He's done everything in his power to keep me safe. If I can let go with anyone, it's right here, with him.

Holding on as tight as I can, I close my eyes and let the sensation take over my body. That white-hot pleasure is spreading, winding its way into my arms and my legs, my fingers and toes, up to the back of my neck where it finally breaks free. A cry rips itself from my throat and my head falls back onto the cold, hard stone, and Lo'zar is fucking me harder and faster than ever as this beautiful agony takes me over. Light fills my vision and I hear him thinking, *Yes, Rimi, yes. Let me have it all.* Each stroke rolls the sensation through me again, picking up even greater steam.

Home. Right here, in Lo'zar's arms, I think I've found home.

I'm so lost to my bliss that when he becomes engorged and full inside me, I'm overcome by it, and my whole body squeezes even tighter. Out loud, Lo'zar gasps my name as he buries himself deep, thrusting into the core of my very being. It sends a final ripple of ecstasy up into my throat, and this time my cry fills up the whole stone room, echoing it back to me, surrounding both of us.

Lo'zar collapses, shivering with the strength of his finish. He brackets my head with his elbows and leans down close, so his nose just grazes mine. I'm still full with him, and my world is spinning so fast I have to shut my eyes.

Lo'zar, I think. *That was wonderful. Like nothing else in the world.* Not only was it the most intense euphoria I've ever experienced in my life... but we also did something powerful and life-changing. It's like I'm a part of him now, and he's a part of me. I wonder if Lo'zar feels the same way.

Good. He kisses my forehead and his tusks scrape my cheeks. *Then I did my job well.*

Chapter 12

Lo'zar

Rimi is so beautiful with her head thrown back and her small mouth taut with pleasure. I want to treat her this way every day as long as she lives. I want to hear her perfect little moans, feel her tight, slippery cunt around me, and keep her wrapped up in my arms, right where she belongs.

I nuzzle her hair, keeping myself propped on one elbow so I don't squish her. My tiny human woman, who I could crush with my body weight. Somehow she took me inside her and loved every moment of it, sobbing out my name as she raced over the precipice with me, hand-in-hand.

But now reality is crashing down around me again. We're trapped under a pile of rocks, waiting and hoping the hunters have given up. If we do get out of here alive, where do we go next where Gusak's riders won't catch up to us? And let's say I can manage to find Rimi a way home. What happens to *me*?

Because now, I don't want to let her go, not ever again.

The rush of this desire takes me by surprise. I've been with many orcesses and trollesses before, but I'm only ever seen as a quick lay, a troll who's easy on the eyes to show them a good time under the blankets. No, Rimi is different. She's special. She's from another world, another plane, sent here with no one to look out for her but me.

I want to stay connected to her as long as possible, so I roll us over with my cock still twitching and throbbing inside her. I could probably get good and ready again for another round without much effort, but this awful floor is hard and cold. I pull Rimi in close and she molds into me, one hand sliding up my tusk. She lets out a deep, contented sigh, and I imagine us lying on a wooden bed draped in furs, a candle burning in a window. I would be most satisfied with someone like her in my blankets every night.

No. I have to get her to safety in human territory, at least, and who knows how long it will take to get there. That's my mission, and I have to finish it.

We should go, I tell Rimi. *Return how we came and try to find a way up the cliffs.* That's our only option.

She doesn't respond. I nudge her forehead to make sure she hasn't fallen asleep, and she glances up at me with wide, curious eyes.

Rimi? What do you think? Again, there's no answer, and I grow concerned. *Can you hear me?* I ask, more frantic. What's happened to the connection between us?

It's as if she's having the same realization. We disengage from each other's bodies, and Rimi sits up on my tunic, worried eyes searching mine.

"Rimi?" I ask. "Can you understand me?"

She blinks and says, "Lo'zar *anya ha saaru?*" Her slender brows crease.

The words don't make sense. It's her voice, but I can't understand her. Icy fear curls in my throat. I can't lose this now that I've just gotten it.

I kiss her forehead to assure her that everything will be all right, and get up to my feet. I tug on my breeches as I walk to the stone in the center of the room, the worms that crawl all over it casting an ethereal glow across Rimi's beautiful, naked body.

There's a small sliver of panic growing in my chest, and by the frightened look on her face, I'm not alone. Perhaps this change wasn't permanent, but temporary—a short boon granted by the strange glowing worms lying at the heart of an ancient ruin.

What will I do if I can't hear Rimi's voice again? If I can't talk to her any longer? I can't stand the thought.

I peer up at the wall where the hands meet between the troll and human faces. What does it mean? I feel like we were meant to find this place, whatever it is. It's some sort of puzzle that I just need to figure out.

"Lo'zar?" Rimi says behind me, voice trembling. She's putting Kugara's tunic on, getting up to her feet without anything covering her cute little thighs. Already I miss being able to tell her everything I'm thinking. She should always know how lovely she is.

The huge stone is shaped like an egg, riddled with holes that the worms use to move through and around it in a constant stream. I lean closer to study them, their four-inch glowing bodies wriggling in a way that would be disgusting if they didn't look like liquid glass. I pick one up, and it frantically tries to get away. Then I turn to Rimi and hold out my hand, gesturing to her with the worm.

My clever human, she understands right away. We did this before, so let's try it again. Rimi eagerly jogs up to the stone and reaches for me. As her palm lands in mine, I wonder what I've found in her.

Just let me hear her voice again, I think, and the worm twitches in our hands.

Lo'zar? I hear Rimi's frantic thoughts. *Can you hear me?*

I can hear you.

She tightens her grip on me and exhales with relief. *Thank goodness. I was so frightened when you didn't...* Her thoughts trail off. *I couldn't stand not being able to talk to you, even for a few moments.*

I know what you mean. Again, the worm shrivels, and the glow inside fades. I drop it to the ground, then put an arm around her shoulders and pull her in. *It felt like I was alone.*

She nods vigorously, wiping at her eyes. *And I don't want to be alone,* she says. *Not ever again.*

What a wonderful creature she is. I want to assure her that she won't be, but I can't possibly know that. Her future is a different one than mine.

How do these things work? I ask, gazing down in wonder at the critters leaving bright, glowing tracks across the stone as they weave in and out of their tunnels. *Both times now, I wished to talk to you. And then it happened.*

Rimi blinks. *It... grants wishes?* She puzzles over this. *But if the wish doesn't last, then we can't leave this place, or we won't be able to hear each other.*

I would rather stay here forever. So I reach out and grab another worm and drop it into my pocket. I'll bring it with me.

Lo'zar! Rimi chides, but she's laughing. *You can't just kidnap one.*

Why not? For good measure, I take a second worm and put it in my other pocket with my fire starter, then a third and a fourth.

Because they'll die. She approaches carrying my tunic, which now carries the pleasant stain of our mutual fluids, and holds it out to me. I'll wear that stain with pride, thank you.

We'll just have to touch one every few hours, I say. *Then we can keep talking. Right?*

Won't we run out eventually? A strange look comes over her. *There might be another way.*

RIMI

There's a myth in Yusala about an ancient beast called Riggamora, whose great long body traversed the world and tore holes in its flesh as it passed, creating many of the rivers and valleys we call home today. Riggamora had achieved its terrible power by devouring humans and trollkin alike and acquiring their magic, thousands of them. The beast grew and grew, using our power against us, until it was finally felled by a true hero.

My parents were always very strict about my diet, because like most Yusalans, they believe everything we let enter our bodies will be returned to us tenfold. You can trap a thing's power inside yourself by consuming it.

So I pick one of the worms up off the rock and wish: *Please let me hear his voice again.* Then I slip it in my mouth.

Lo'zar makes a horrible *gyechh!* sound as it slides past my lips. His face is aghast. The worm wriggles as I try to get my throat to open for it, and I might throw up—but I manage to swallow the worm all the way down until I can feel it wriggling in my belly.

What... What did you just do? Lo'zar asks with extreme uncertainty.

What did it look like? I reach out, grab another worm, and offer it to him. *If only touching it gives us this kind of power, imagine if you let it become a part of you.*

He blinks, perplexed. *Let it become a part of me?*

So many things are different in this part of the world. I wonder if the trollkin even know about the legend of Riggamora.

Yes. I hold out the worm, and reluctantly, Lo'zar takes it. *Consuming it might make the effects last longer.*

Longer. Maybe not forever, but it would give us more time before the gift fades away again.

Looking suspiciously at the worm, Lo'zar brings it to his lips, then gives me one more wary look. I nod my head encouragingly.

This way you can keep saying nice things to me while you're inside me, I say, and my face gets hot just thinking the words.

A big grin sweeps across Lo'zar's face. Without hesitation, he chants his own wish, then sucks the worm down in one motion. There's a slurping sound as it vanishes into his mouth and down his throat. He gags and coughs.

Tastes like... worm, he says, wiping his face, and I laugh.

Should we experiment and see if it lasts this time? I don't know when I became so forward. Maybe it happened the moment he slipped his cock inside me and I understood what it could feel like. Maybe it happened when I looked into his eyes and saw him in there, all of him, and realized that I was meant to find him.

We should, Lo'zar says, his hand traveling to my hip, then dipping beneath my tunic. There's a wickedness in his eyes as four fingers reach up and brush my nipple. Immediately I want him all over me.

This time he takes me from behind, running his hands up and down my back as he slides in and out, drawing my pleasure along as far as it will go. It's as if he knows my body already and everything it wants. When I cry out and clench up tight around him, he bellows and rams himself deep. I desire all of him. I will suck him dry.

LO'ZAR

When my Rimi is finally spent, all I want is to fall asleep, but I have to stay alert in case the hunters finally find their way down here.

Lo'zar? Rimi's mental voice says. *Can you still hear me?*

I can hear you.

An uneasiness creeps into her tone. *Maybe it's time to leave now.*

I don't know how long our gift will last this time, but I hope a very long time. Now that I can hear all of Rimi's sweet words, I never want to stop.

When we stand up, I get that strange feeling again, like this is all very familiar—but with it comes a deep, ugly sense of dread that makes my hair stand up.

I think they're coming, Rimi says, and her hand finds its way into mine. She's scared of something.

I thought it was just in my head. *You feel that, too?*

She nods furiously. *We have to get out of here.*

But where? I look back up at the stairs leading down into this massive room. The only way in or out.

That's when I feel that strange sensation again, the one that drew me downward to find this place. It's nagging at me, urging me to get beneath this floor somehow.

It gives me the creeps, if I'm being honest.

I think we need to go down, I tell her. *I don't know how I know, but I do.*

But where? Rimi furrows her brow in thought, then looks at the floor. She walks around the room, searching for something, but I don't know what. Maybe she doesn't know, either. I do the same thing on the other side, hoping to find a secret trap door in the stone. But everything looks the same—unmarked, scratched up, old. All I find is a skeletal snake, and my dread grows.

Returning to the rock in the middle of the room, I let out a groan of frustration. Down? Down where? I lean against it, racking my brain for an answer.

Underneath me, the rock moves.

Huh? I push it harder, and it moves a little bit more, then a little more. There's something underneath it—a dark hole. Sweat dots my forehead, and my skin feels too cold. We're running out of time. I push with everything I have, and sure enough, it reveals a cavern underneath. This is our chance to get out of here before they come.

As if I've summoned them with my thoughts, the hunters burst out of the tunnel up above us in a thunder of footsteps. When they spot us down below, the three roar in unison. Their eyes glow the same purple as the magic worms.

"Lo'zar!" Rimi cries out as the hunters split up and head down the stairs. She races towards me as I reach for my gun with one hand and my sword with the other. When the first hunter is within range, I fire the loaded round, and my bullet eats through the leopard pelt hanging around his shoulders, striking him in the chest. Blood spurts out, and he stumbles and falls to the ground in a heap. The one behind him simply jumps over his body as if he isn't there.

Rimi! I call out. *Hide underneath this rock!*

What?! She's incredulous. *I'm not leaving you here!*

The hunters close in on me in a pincer formation, one from each side. I have two more rounds on me, but no time to load one. I put the gun away and two-hand my sword, thinking that perhaps I can take both of them on at the same time if I'm fast and careful. But the fearless bloodlust on their faces does give me some doubt.

Then a tiny purple worm goes flying through the air, over my head. When it lands on the ground in front of the closest hunter...

It explodes with an ear-shattering *boom*.

Chapter 13

If the worms can let us speak to each other, what else can they do? I have to save Lo'zar. I can't let him face these mad trolls alone. He won't survive.

Please help him, I think hard. *Please stop those monsters.*

And then I hurl the worm as hard as I can.

When it explodes, Lo'zar goes flying backwards, slamming into the rock. *Shit!* While he's trying to get his breath back, I grab onto him, pulling him as hard as I can toward the hole in the floor. I don't know where it leads, but perhaps he can hide there until I've taken out the hunters.

Go, I snap when he resists. *I'll hold them off.*

Lo'zar looks like he wants to argue, but I push him away as I grab another worm, reel back my arm, and throw it. There's an earth-shaking explosion on the other side of the room.

Then, from all around us comes a terrible noise. Grumbling. Shifting. Rocks upon rocks starting to move, everywhere.

"Rimi!" Lo'zar shouts. *The pyramid, it's going to come down!*

But those damn hunters are still coming for us, covered in their comrade's blood and their own, glowing eyes shining out from underneath it.

I told you to go! I holler back at him. Grabbing the torch off the floor, Lo'zar finally does what I ask and jumps into the cavern underneath us. I pick up yet another worm and hurl it, wishing again, *Stop them. Kill them.*

There's another immense bang that seems to rattle every last stone in the pyramid. That's when the first rock falls from the ceiling. One crashes into the stone floor with a terrible sound, and the whole pyramid shakes.

Rimi! Lo'zar is calling to me, one hand outstretched. *Come on! Please!*

Another massive stone tumbles down, then another. It's collapsing right on top of us.

I have no choice. I leap down into the cavern, landing in Lo'zar's arms. He clutches me tight as the ground shakes and trembles.

Overhead, there's a deep groaning sound. The stone above us is moving again of its own volition. The worms swarm over it, faster and faster, their bodies leaving glowing purple tracks in and out of their tunnels.

Just as the ceiling starts to collapse, the hunters screaming, the stone closes—leaving us in darkness.

Whoa, I say as it snaps into place, and a deafening roar fills the air: a cacophony of rocks tumbling down as the ancient structure crumbles. The stone walls around us shake, and I cling to Lo'zar, hoping that they don't give way to the pressure.

We stay like that in the darkness, huddled together, until the terrible rumbling finally stops.

Uneasily, Lo'zar releases me. He feels around on the ground, his hands running over my feet as he looks for something. Then he goes, *A-ha!* and his fire-starter snaps as it lights the torch.

He holds up the flame, revealing a cramped cave. It looks like it was here already, but somebody carved it to be usable. It continues on ahead, narrower, and the sight of that infinite blackness makes my chest seize.

This isn't just a crate. There are no vent holes here, no lid to be pried off. We are buried.

What is this place? I ask, gazing around us as I wrap my arms around myself. The worms are pulsing inside the rock over our heads, unmoving.

I don't know. But we were given a gift. We should take it. Lo'zar gestures on ahead of us. *Let's go.*

I look down into the darkness, then behind us again at the sealed-off hole, and images flick past of infinite days trapped in the crate, swaying with the boat. But we have no choice except to go forward.

We set off down the narrow tunnel, Lo'zar walking behind me with the torch held up. I'm not surprised to find more markings on the wall with the same strange humanoid shapes as before. As the path descends even deeper, I try not to let the seed of fear in me grow into something bigger. But the walls are closing in around me. Will I ever see the light of day again?

As if he knows what's happening in my mind, Lo'zar puts a gentle, reassuring hand on my shoulder, and I become stronger knowing he's with me. No matter what happens, if Lo'zar is at my side, I'll be safe.

So we walk, down and down, and I wonder if it will lead us straight to the center of the earth. What lies this far beneath the surface? Perhaps this tunnel was dug by one of the great worms I read about, and then taken over by whoever built all of this.

Luckily, soon we reach an equilibrium—and after a while further of walking, the path tilts back toward the surface again.

It will be all right, Rimi, Lo'zar says, stroking my back as we walk, and I'm immensely glad we haven't lost our connection to one another yet.

How did you know to push that stone? I ask as we follow the tunnel. How far does it go? I hope it's a way out, and not a tomb.

No, I can't think like that.

It was just a feeling, he says. *How did you know to throw those worms?* He grins and elbows me. *That was slick.*

I told them what I desired. Whatever was inside those worms, the magic that was imbued in them… *Magic,* I say as the realization strikes me. *I think what we found back there was magic. And it's very powerful, at least it is in all the legends we have in Yusala. We could do all sorts of things with it once upon a time, for better or worse.*

We? Lo'zar asks.

Sure. Trollkin and humans both, at least back then. I hum thoughtfully. *I thought those were all just stories. But maybe magic was real.*

That's when, up ahead, I see that the path abruptly ends. I reach it and look all around us, but there's no other way to go.

We're stuck! As I imagine the collapsed pyramid blocking our way out on the other end, my breathing speeds up. We can't be trapped down here in the darkness, where there's no difference between sleeping and waking. I can't die like this, squeezed in from all sides. *Lo'zar,* I whimper, *we're—!*

Hey. He stops me with a hand on my waist. *It's all right. Look up.*

I let his voice bring me back, and obediently glance upward as he holds out the torch. High overhead the stone wall continues up, with indents that look like hand-holds.

We have to climb out, he says. He sets down the torch, then picks me up and lifts me toward the hand-holds. *Grab on.*

What about you? I ask.

I'll be fine. Go. I hook my hand onto the nearest cleft in the stone, but my grip is weak and my fingers are tired from holding tight onto Lo'zar's neck on our run through the jungle. I struggle to hang on, so he pushes me up further. Finally, I can get my feet into the lower indentations, too, and begin crawling my way up the wall. But I can't see what's ahead of me, not with Lo'zar holding the torch down on the ground.

I continue to climb up into the darkness, hoping against hope that our way out hasn't been sealed over. What if so many hundreds or thousands of years have passed that it's no longer an escape?

Suddenly, my head bumps into something, and I flinch.

There's something here, I tell him. I nudge whatever it is with my head again, and it gives way. I carefully remove one hand from my tenuous hold on the wall, and reach up to push. I feel soft earth, and as I claw at it, some of it falls. *Watch out!*

Then the ceiling collapses, and I have to hang on as piles of dirt fall on top of me and past me. Down below, I hear Lo'zar curse something in Trollkin, and the torch goes out. But that's not a problem now, because fresh, real sunlight is streaming inside from above. My heart leaps at the sight of the sun, my oldest friend.

Light! Lo'zar says. *That must be the way out!*

Frantically I reach up and grab the edge of the hole that's appeared over my head, then pull myself as hard as I can. My fingers are scrabbling at the mud and branches, but I bunch up my muscles as tight as I can and then, I'm climbing out. I fall onto the jungle floor, panting, bathed in warm daylight.

I finally get back up to my feet, but before I can look back down into the hole, Lo'zar springs out of it, and I shriek and fall backwards. With a laugh, he reaches down to help me up.

Sorry. I throw my arms around him and he pulls me in tight. Lo'zar kisses my hair, then tilts my face up so he can look in my eyes. *We made it.*

I stand up on my tip-toes and plant a kiss on his lips, and Lo'zar returns it eagerly. Soon he's assaulting my mouth with such ferocity that I have to hold onto one of his tusks. Eventually, he pulls away. *We should figure out where we are.*

I nod in agreement. I don't know where we go next, but at least we're alive and safe, and I never have to see the inside of that dark pit ever again.

CHAPTER 14

LO'ZAR

We're free.

I'm not sure where we are, but we made it out of that damn pyramid alive, though not without some casualties. And somehow, we're back in the jungle, almost as if by magic.

Magic. I wonder if Rimi is right. Those glowing worms, the moving stone... None of it makes rational sense. Something about that place was beyond this world. And that instinct I had that led us downward, that got us out safely?

I don't know, but I can't help feeling it was much greater than us, like we are simply two cogs in an ancient machine. Surely Rimi is right, and we found something out of legend down there.

Lo'zar? Rimi asks, searching my face. *Can you still hear me?*

I nod quickly. *Yes. I was just thinking about...* We don't have time for this right now. *It doesn't matter. We should get moving.* I try to get a sense of where the sun is, but it's hard to make out through the dense jungle.

There. It's getting low in the sky—must be afternoon. *That's west,* I say, pointing off through the trees. *Let's go that way for a while and see what happens.*

She thinks this through, then nods in agreement. Let's get oriented around something familiar and go from there.

All right, she says. *At least then we'll have a heading.*

I don't know what comes next once we find it, but I do know that together Rimi and I can come up with a plan. We'll need to be quick about it, though, with all the supplies back at the wagon where we left it.

We walk through the jungle for what feels like hours as the sun creeps lower. Maybe I was wrong. What if the tunnel brought us out somewhere totally different than where we went in?

What are you thinking about? Rimi asks, reaching out to take my hand. She's watching my face carefully. Always alert, always studying. My crafty human.

What that place was. What happened there. She turns away in embarrassment, and I let out a guffaw. *That, too.*

It was uncanny, right? she says. *I'm not the only one who thought it was incredibly odd?*

Nothing about that entire experience was normal, I say. *Except the part where I fucked you twice.*

The pink in her face turns bright red. *That's so crass!* She pretends to look offended, but under it she's grinning.

What else would you call it? I ask, enjoying myself as I watch her grow more and more flustered.

I can't believe we destroyed an ancient pyramid, she finally says. *What have we done?*

We got out alive, I say, squeezing her tiny fingers in my palm. *And that's what matters.*

The road appears out of nowhere. One moment we're walking through trees, and the next the jungle's given way.

I search up and down the road, hoping I'll recognize where we are. *The way is clear,* I tell her.

Which direction? Rimi asks, peering around me.

I try to remember what the map looked like for those few moments I saw it. The road wound its way to the northwest, so if we had to walk that far to get here, we must be towards the south. I try to calculate this in my head.

That way is the city, I say, pointing to the left. Then I gesture right. *That way is the wagon.*

Well, we should definitely get back to the wagon. That's where all your stuff is, right? We need food.

But I'm not so sure. If we're as far south as I think we are...

Shit. Grabbing her hand, we dive back into the trees.

What is it?

Gusak's men. They'll be coming this way, right along this road, any time now.

Is Gusak the guy you work for? Rimi asks.

Worked for, I correct her. Now I'd be lucky if I didn't get tossed into the ring with one of his best prize fighters and beaten to death in front of an audience. But looking down at Rimi's pretty black hair and soft, small face, it was a very worthwhile trade. I wouldn't change anything. *He's going to be looking for us.*

Then something occurs to me. Gusak's riders will be expecting to see us far on ahead, in the direction we went with the wagon after abandoning Kugara and Drozeg. They'll be running at full speed, trying to catch up—not looking along the path this close to Kalishagg.

After handling the hunters, I have faith we can outsmart Gusak, too.

I know exactly how to get to safety, and perhaps, even get Rimi back home: right underneath the boss's nose.

Rimi

We have to walk for how long? I ask, dragging my tired feet another long step.

It will probably take us three or four days on foot.

I groan and sag against a tree. I'm exhausted, hungry, and tired. Sleeping on the hard stone was not the restorative night's rest one would hope for. Once again I'm longing for my big, soft bed back home.

I try to imagine Lo'zar in that bed with me, but the ideas don't fit together. He would never belong in my prim and proper mansion.

I don't need to think about that right now. His plan is to go right back into the lion's den—return to the city where his "clan" is located, and sneak me onto a ship out. *They won't be looking for us there,* he'd said. *All his spare hands will be out riding through the jungle.*

I have to admit that it's a good plan, but also a dangerous one.

Finally, I ask a question that's been burning in my mind since I was kidnapped. *Lo'zar,* I say. *Where were you taking me? Before you let me go?*

His jaw clenches, like he doesn't want to answer. *You were sold,* he finally says. *I was delivering you to the buyer.*

The buyer? A shiver slides down my arms. *For what?*

Who knows. He shakes his head vehemently. *But whoever bought a little human didn't have good intentions.*

I imagine what those intentions might be, and my stomach turns like I've drunk sour milk. Surely I would have been used in some terrible way. My monumental appreciation for Lo'zar washes over me, and all I want is to pay him back for everything he's sacrificed.

Thank you, I say finally. *I don't know if I've told you that yet. But what you did for me—*

Shh. He nudges me with his elbow. *You don't have to thank me. You didn't ask to be kidnapped and brought here. I did what I knew I had to do, and I'd do it again.*

Tears threaten at the back of my eyes. My troll is good. Very good.

Eventually I have to stop to lean on a tree and take a breather, then I slide down so I'm sitting on the ground. *I just need some rest*, I say. The sun has practically gone down already.

Lo'zar takes a look around us like he's just realizing how dark it is. *We can stop for the night.* He pulls out his gun and looks off into the woods. *I have two rounds left. I'll try to find us some dinner.* He looks down at me. *Do you know how to make a fire?*

I'm so useless. I can't hunt or make fires or anything. I've spent my life in a nice house with all of my needs attended to by maids and cooks.

I shake my head. *Sorry. But if you tell me what to get, I'll get it.*

He explains to me about dry moss and dead branches and I start looking while he wanders off into the woods. We put a big stick straight up in the ground so we know where to return to.

Once I've found plenty of the things we need, I make my way back to the spot. Out in the woods I hear a *bang!* and then Lo'zar lets out a cackle. He's like a boy sometimes... while very much a man in other ways.

A troll, I guess. My silly, excitable troll.

He returns a while later carrying a small deer, and I recoil at the blood leaking from its wound. But Lo'zar doesn't notice my expression as he drops the deer in front of me and surveys the pile of materials I brought him.

Good. This will make a nice fire. We're a long way off the main road, so he doesn't seem nervous about lighting one. He assembles all the sticks and moss into a little tent shape that reminds me of the pyramid, then uses his fire starter to light the moss. It quickly catches, and I try to commit this process to memory for tomorrow.

Find some big sticks, he instructs me, and pulls out his sword. He slices into the deer, drawing dark blood, and I turn away.

Right. Big sticks. I head off into the trees, hoping I can still find my way back in the dark. The moon is already rising overhead, but very little of it makes it down through the canopy.

I grab a few large sticks, then return to find Lo'zar has most of the small animal butchered, and his sword is drenched in blood. I feel a little sick to my stomach as I show him the sticks, and he takes them, spearing each piece of meat and holding it over the fire. It's pathetic how little experience I have with where my food comes from. He gives me a stick to hold, too, and shows me how to turn it a little at a time to cook the meat.

Usually, I have a gadget for this, he says. *It was back at the wagon.* He explains how his friend Graz built it, so it folds out and becomes a nice little structure over the fire that's perfect for cooking food. Halfway through telling me this, he stops abruptly.

Graz, he says. *Maybe Graz can help us.*

Who?

My friend. He thinks about this for a while. *Yeah. That's what we'll do. He'll know how to get you home.*

Home. I know that's what I want—to be with my family again, as strange as life with them is. I want to sleep in my bed, to wander the garden grounds and swim in the lake. To be safe, to never fear the crate.

But as Lo'zar chatters on, I feel a hard tug in my chest. Leaving this strange continent means leaving him, too. Maybe I've only known him for a few days, but I feel a bond I've never experienced with anyone before. I want all of him, always. That big grin, the devilish handsomeness, his cheeky charm; the way he cares about me and protects me like I'm the most precious thing in the world to him.

Rimi? Lo'zar has stopped talking and is watching me curiously.

Sorry. I'm just thinking about home.

His face falls, and I realize how crude that sounds. Instead of being here with him, he thinks my mind is off in the sky, back in Yusala.

Don't worry. He forces on a carefree smile. *We'll get you there.*

I suppose that's what I should want. This place is temporary, and most of my time here was a nightmare. My parents must miss me immensely. Do they think I'm dead? Perhaps we never had a close relationship, but surely they want me home again, where I belong.

I wonder if they've buried me.

Lo'zar is quiet after that, lost in his own thoughts. I run a finger down his arm to get his attention, and start tapping on the wooden cooking stick in my hand. I want to raise his spirits again, remind him that I'm here with him. He raises an eyebrow at me, and one tusk slides high up on his face as he grins. With his own stick he taps on the ground in the same regular rhythm, until we're both drumming along with the beat. Then Lo'zar jangles his rings together, adding another layer of sound. I slide closer, and tap my nails on his sword, which lets out a metallic ring. My troll's grin widens. Soon we're tapping out a song, just the two of us alone in the jungle, with no one around to interrupt us. And despite everything, I think this is the happiest I've ever been.

Suddenly Lo'zar stops. He wraps one arm behind my neck, pulling me in close for a kiss. It isn't the urgent, devouring kiss I was expecting, though. It's slow and sensual as he sucks on my lower lip, and smooths over it with his tongue. In it is everything he feels about me, and the tenderness makes my heart want to break open and spill out all over the ground.

When he finally pulls away, Lo'zar brings me under his arm and squeezes me to his side, leaning his face into my hair. Maybe we're on the run, and it looks like danger is around every corner, but I almost don't want to return to civilization.

What if we just lived out here, in the jungle, wild and free?

But I know that can't happen. Lo'zar had a life before me, before he sacrificed everything to help me.

After we've cleaned up our meal, it's time to try to sleep on the jungle floor. It's even worse than the inside of the pyramid, with sticks and stones digging into my back everywhere I try to lie down.

Feeling anxious? he asks.

I'm ashamed just saying it. *I don't know how to sleep on the ground.*

His grin is big. *I know a cure for that.* He picks me up around the middle, then rolls us over so I'm sitting on his hips. He draws me down onto him, tucking my head under his chin. *There. Use me as a bed, princess Rimi.*

Princess?! He laughs that big, boisterous laugh, and I cuddle close to his chest. His arms wrap tight around me, and if I weren't so exhausted, I would try to rouse the delightful creature that lies between Lo'zar's very shapely legs. Instead I close my eyes and listen to the slow beating of his huge heart, and let it lull me to sleep.

CHAPTER 15

I check a few times a day that we're still going alongside the road, but for the most part, we stay deep in the jungle, hoping to avoid Gusak's riders. Rimi's stomach grumbles constantly. Just one big meal at dinnertime isn't enough for her small human body, which seems to need nutrients much more often, but the meat would've gone bad if we'd tried to bring it with us. That afternoon, I find some tiny red fruits high up in the trees, and climb up to knock them down for her. Rimi lets out a squeal of delight as they tumble to the ground, only a few landing in her open hands.

We take as many as we can, bundling them up in big leaves and carrying them under both arms.

Though we're tired and hungry, I'm happy as can be at her side. She counts as she hops over little ferns, and stares up into the trees with wonder when a huge, colorful bird flies overhead. I love the way she hums under her breath, usually some little ditty I don't recognize. I ask her to teach me a song, because it sounds beautiful, but that might just be because it's falling from her lips.

It's a folk song in Yusala, she says. She repeats the tune for me, and I sing it back to her with bravado. She laughs and claps her hands. *You have a nice voice, Lo'zar.*

Thank you. I lean down and brush over her ear with one tusk. *So do you. And I plan to make you sing quite a lot later.*

Her whole body shudders at my suggestion, and I'm pleased that I can do this to her. All it takes is a sweep of my hand over her hip and she's leaning into me, telling me with her body how much she wants me, and it floods my head with a giddiness I haven't felt since I fucked someone the first time.

We continue to sing the song as we march through the jungle, arms linked together while we carry our fruit along with us. She adds words and I try to repeat them, but I must be mangling it because Rimi laughs uproariously.

What does it mean? I ask. It's so strange that I can't understand her tongue, and yet I can hear her voice as clear as if she were speaking my own language.

It's about the beginning, before Riggamora. She taps her chin thoughtfully. *Actually, it's a love story.*

A love story?

About a woman who could wield magic and her forbidden lover.

I quirk an eyebrow. She must be yanking my chain.

The thought seems to occur to Rimi at the same moment, because her eyebrows go high up into her hair. Then she gives me a sly look. *Does that make you my forbidden lover?* she asks.

I would worship her body, kiss her sweet-tasting lips, and bury my cock in her every day and night if I could—but I know that's not allowed to me. This has been a fun game between us, but she's a human, and I know it can't possibly last.

I suppose I am.

But when we "rest" for the night, I can pretend, just for a while, that we are the people in the song. Like the magic woman and her lover, we can change the world to suit ourselves.

I manage to trap one of those big, loud birds for us to eat, and Rimi covers her eyes as I butcher it in front of her. She is delicate, my girl. Despite everything that's happened to her, it hasn't corrupted that kind, earnest innocence she has inside.

Thank you, Rimi says out of the blue as she licks another tiny bird bone clean.

For what? I still enjoy the fact that I can eat and talk at the same time.

For everything. She picks up another bone. *You're feeding me. You saved me. You've given up… a lot for me.* Her eyes fall at this. *I'm sorry. Now you can't go home because of me, too.*

I reach out and take her chin in my hand, urging her to look at me. Those gray eyes are sweet and as mysterious as the moon, and I wonder again who sent her to me. *That was a choice I made,* I tell her firmly. *I did what I did because I wanted to. Because… you're worth it. More than worth it.*

She makes a choked sound, and I gently take the food out of her hands so I can pull her in my arms. Rimi buries her face in my neck, leaving a wet spot there.

I don't know what I did to deserve you, she says.

I've been thinking the same thing. I'm not a good guy. I shouldn't have been given a gift like you.

Her hands tighten into fists in my shirt, and she pulls away to glare at me. *You're a wonderful guy,* she says, her eyebrows pulled together tight. *The best one I've ever met.*

By the certainty in her voice, I can almost believe her. But she doesn't know me, not really. All she knows is the troll I've shown her.

I haven't told you the kinds of things I've done. And I don't want to. I want Rimi's picture of me to be the knight in shining armor she imagines me to be.

She puts her hands on each of my tusks, pulling my face in so I have to look her right in the eyes.

It doesn't matter what you've done, she says, leaning her forehead against mine. Her hands turn soft as she strokes one tusk. *It matters who you are inside, and I know that troll.*

I shake my head. I've spent my life stealing, taking what isn't mine so I can survive—so I can thrive. I've killed, more than once, sometimes without hesitation or remorse. But my Rimi doesn't need to know all that.

Lo'zar. Her hands travel down my jaw to my throat, my shoulders, my sides, like she's memorizing how I feel. *There's a reason we ended up in that pyramid, that we found that magic down there.* She takes my hand in hers and squeezes it. *The same reason it was you outside that cage. Because only you would have freed me.*

Even though we're on the run now, I feel certain that Rimi has freed me, too.

I pull her in tight, wrapping her roughly in my arms, our food forgotten. *I wonder what that reason is*, I say. *What those faces were.* The human and the trollkin staring into each other's eyes... I feel that way now as I gaze at Rimi, where all I can see is her.

Maybe, she says cautiously, *we aren't the only ones.* She trails a finger down my cheek, looking deeply into me. *What if others have found what we did down there? Or... what if they left it for us to find?*

It's strange to think. For all of our history as I know it, humans and trollkin have killed one another for food, for land, simply for existing. It was a mark of victory in the village where I grew up to have a trinket from a dead human—we hung up their weapons as trophies, the pride of an enemy slain. We sang songs around the fire about the brave warriors who had fought to keep them out of our territory.

So how could there be this path between us, written thousands of years ago on an ancient stone wall? It would seem senseless if it weren't for the way everything with Rimi makes perfect sense. Her mouth on mine, her small face in my big palms... It's all just how it's supposed to be. Rimi's body relaxes against me, giving to me, and I want nothing more than to surround her, tuck her in close, and keep her safe from everything in this big wide world that might try to harm her or take her from me.

Her hands roam just as freely, ducking under my shirt, skating over my nipples and then stopping to play with the piercings there. *Oh, damn*, I think, and Rimi chuckles. No one's done that to me before and made it feel so good. It's like there's a ribbon stretched between us, where every one of her pleasures and mine reverberate, rising in intensity the more we touch.

I think we can agree on one thing, I tell her, enthralled that I can still talk to her while I devour her lips. *I was meant to find you.*

Her shirt comes off easily over her tiny body, and I lay it flat on the ground along with mine. I won't have my little Rimi all scratched up by the jungle floor. But she's upright and eager, and once we're both blissfully naked, she crawls into my lap, my cock wedged between us. Oh, does it enjoy her, already weeping at the tip as I imagine what it will feel like to be inside her again. She takes it in her small hands, and I groan as her fingers explore down beneath, where she discovers my balls. I love the way her grey eyes glitter as she massages them, earning a groan from me. Soon she's stroking in both places at the same time, watching my face intently as I jerk underneath her. This is what my dreams look like. Rimi could lead me to a cliff and I would jump off it for her.

I guess I have already.

When I'm least expecting it, she leans down and brings her mouth to the round head of my cock. *Rimi?* I ask with surprise.

But she doesn't answer, and takes me in her lips instead. I moan as I slip inside that wet, warm place, and her tongue goes right to dancing around me.

You did this for me, she says wickedly, *and it felt lovely, so I bet it will feel good for you, too.*

I chuckle. *Oh, it does, princess. It does.*

I'm almost over the edge again when I have the sense to stop her. She gives me a questioning look, so I draw her hands up to my face, kissing each one in turn.

If you keep that up, I tell her in a serious tone, *then I won't be able to fuck you as many times as I want.*

And that's a lot of times? she asks, lips twitching with mischief.

Whatever is 'a lot,' it's even more than that.

Chapter 16

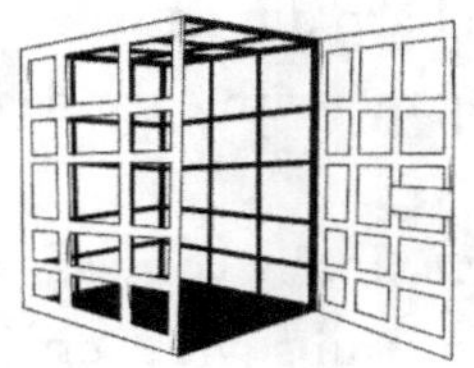

Rimi

I love all of Lo'zar's little promises, and each one makes me surer of him than the last one.

He is good. He may be a mischief-maker, and lived a rough life, but his soul is made of spun gold. I want to hold it in my hands and blow on it gently, like a small flame, and bring it to life. So I wrap my arms around his neck, holding him tight, and lift my hips until his cock is right underneath me. His eyes widen, and I like surprising him this way.

But I'm learning not to dive in fast. No, Lo'zar draws it out, and that's what makes it so much better than that crass stablehand. I kneel around his hips as his cock settles right between my thighs, the shaft pressed against that slick, hot place. I find it easy to slide back and forth, rubbing my clit against his head, then just teasing what it might feel like to take him inside me. His hips buck with each stroke, and he gasps my name.

So it's like that, is it? Lo'zar asks, bringing his hands to my hips and pressing me down even harder, grinding me against his cock. *You want to ride me, do you?*

I have always been good on horseback, I say, and Lo'zar lets out a guffaw. He reaches down between us while I pleasure myself, and seeks the tiny pearl hidden in my folds. Now it's my turn to writhe as he passes over it again and again, grinning up at me as I tease his cockhead with that sharp dip between my thighs. He drags me back and forth, sampling me with each pass, then retaking my lips and devouring them.

I can't take any more, I finally confess, and Lo'zar grins against my mouth. He hefts up my hips with very little effort—sometimes I forget how small I am compared to him—and holds me there, where all he would need to do is lower me an inch and his beautiful cock would slip right inside. I reach down and spread myself with my fingers for him, and with a hungry groan, he sinks into me.

Oh, how that fat head squeezes in, forcing me wide open for him. I gasp and grip him hard around the neck.

Too fast? he asks, a tinge of concern in his voice.

I shake my head. No, I want more, if anything. I want all of him. *Please*, I say. *I need you, Lo'zar.*

He grins that wide, charming grin, and releases his tight hold on my ass. The sensation of him filling me up again wrenches a moan from my throat, and locked together this way, I finally feel complete. This is where he belongs, where *I* belong.

Once he's as deep inside me as he can go, I lean my forehead against his, panting heavily as I adjust to him. It feels like my entire body is shifting to accommodate, making room for him, swallowing him as much as it can.

"Rimi," he says in a whisper. *You feel incredible. Amazing. Perfect.*

I clutch his braid in my hand as I try to steady myself. *You do, too. Like everything I've ever wanted but I didn't know it.* He captures my lips in his, nipping them with his teeth and soothing them over with his tongue.

I know what you mean.

Slowly, I lift my hips, rising until his cock almost slips out of me, then I sink back down. The sensation of him is blistering, sweet and thick and so flawless I think I might cry. He grips my ass firmly with his four fingers, lending me his strength as I continue to move up and down, faster and faster, until my breasts are bouncing and we're both crying out our pleasure. He seizes my nipples, tormenting them as I take him, sending sharp ripples of bliss through my bloodstream.

I've never felt anything like what Lo'zar makes me feel. I love his big, curved tusks, his orange eyes, his thick hair. I love his purple-blue skin, and how tough and sturdy he feels under my hands. All of it heightens the joy of having him inside me, of being connected.

Wrapping his arms around me, he presses me down so I'm underneath him, and the change in angle makes me squirm and moan. Now in control of our speed, Lo'zar strokes in and out at a smooth, slow pace, making sure I can feel every last inch of him fully. I bury my face in his shoulder, clutching him close as his body speaks to mine, both of them united for our singular purpose of being together. Heat builds in my abdomen, a tingling that grows and grows, spidering out across my body. I shudder and cry out as it overtakes me, and I'm squeezing him tight with my arms and legs and pussy all at once. He groans, his tusks brushing my cheeks with every one of his thrusts.

Fuck, he says, and it's accompanied by another sharp breath. *I can't believe I found you.* He works faster inside me, driven on by my rising volume, seeking out my innermost being, and that agonizing pleasure has grown so big and so volcanically hot that I almost can't take it.

Please, please, please, I think, feeling like I might just spring apart.

Yes, my troll says, holding my body firmly under his as he plunders me. *Come for me.*

On command, my body releases. It's like flying and falling at the same time, and a warm darkness envelops me as it takes over. I scream and clench, gripping his waist so tight with my thighs that the muscles seize. Lo'zar's heavy breathing takes on a frantic pitch as he fucks me through my orgasm. His voice joins mine, and through his mind I hear a jumble of pleasure and prayer and joy. It sends me careening even further into the abyss, and tears are streaming from my eyes as I finally crash and hit the ground.

We lie there panting, our sweat mixing together as we rest forehead-to-forehead. There are so many big words bubbling up to the surface inside me, but I keep them out of my conscious thoughts. They are too sincere, too frightening for Lo'zar to hear them.

Something in my soul has shifted and changed course. I hold him as tight as I can.

Lo'zar

When I lie on top of her, my seed dripping from her tiny cunt onto the jungle floor, I think that I've found something I didn't even know I was looking for. It's as if I were cut into a shape at birth, Rimi given the same one in reverse, and now we've found each other. We fit together like it was always meant to be that way.

I fall asleep with my arm wrapped around her, relishing the smell of her, and thinking how despite the disaster that's followed us, I wouldn't change anything.

The next day, it's hard not to consider my future. *Our* future.

I know that this is going to end. What we have won't last—but all my instincts rebel hard against this thought. She should be here with me, forever. Maybe I can't fill her up with whelp or watch her get big and round, but I want the chance to try. I want to give her a life where I can always bring fresh food home to her, where she has a soft place to sleep, where we can keep exploring this strange and wonderful connection we have.

Now that I've found her, my person, my human... I can't imagine watching her leave me behind.

But I have to. She is like a beautiful wild animal who doesn't belong here in captivity. She needs to go home where she can truly thrive, instead of living in fear of discovery and ending up in a cage again.

And I'm a fugitive from one of the biggest criminal clans in the trollkin empire. They'll always be sniffing around for me. I can't put her at risk like that, too.

You're quiet today, Rimi says as we walk, like she can read my mind. I guess she kind of can. I have to be careful about the thoughts I put into words.

I'm just strategizing. I'm so grateful we haven't lost the ability to communicate. I don't know what I'd do. I guess I would learn the human tongue just so I could keep talking to her and learning her mind.

Oh. She doesn't sound like she believes me, but she lets it drop. It doesn't feel right lying to her, but I know what has to be done. I don't need to saddle her with my worries.

That's when, over the tops of the trees, I catch a glimpse of the Grand Chieftain's tower. We're here at last, and one step closer to getting Rimi home.

I've debated how to get past the guards at the gates of Kalishagg with a human in tow, without raising the alarm and drawing Gusak's attention. Unfortunately, there's just one way to pull it off—even then, it puts us at high risk of discovery.

I've got a plan, I tell her. *But it's risky.*

Everything we've done until now has been risky. She gets a mischievous glint in her eye. *I trust you.*

My daring Rimi. I grab her hand and suddenly pull her against me, wrapping my arms tight around her tiny body. She lets out a squeak, then relaxes into me. When she tries to hold me in return, her small hands only reach partway around my waist.

What is it? she asks.

Nothing. I kiss the top of her head, then rub my cheek against it, getting some of her hair caught around my tusk. I can't get enough of her. I want to tell her how I feel—that we have united, that we're supposed to be together as determined by some power greater than us—but she wants to go home, and she doesn't need to be looking back.

It's time to go and attempt my foolhardy plan.

RIMI

I know that Lo'zar is lying to me. I don't know *how* I know, but I do. It's in his voice, his touch, the way his heart is beating hard and fast in his chest while I press my face against it.

Doesn't he feel this, too? This bone-deep awareness that we were supposed to find each other, that what we share is something special, something one-of-a-kind, and we could be the luckiest beings on earth to have discovered it?

But he's so eager to help me get home that he'll risk returning to this city, where he's a wanted troll. That's what I want, too—to live in my own world, to return to my parents and tell them I'm all right. I don't want to worry about hiding in the back of carts, fearing discovery, wondering if I'll get captured and sold off again.

And I don't want to be a burden on Lo'zar, either, any longer than necessary. He's already put himself on the line so many times to protect me, and I can't keep asking that of him, not when he's already on the run and trying to save his own hide.

I'm going to tie you up, Lo'zar says, searching the trees for something. He locates a vine and tears it down. *You'll have to pretend to be my prisoner.*

It makes sense, of course, but it also means becoming a captive again. I wring my hands, biting back bile. *They won't take me from you, will they?*

Don't worry. He stoops down to kiss the top of my head. *I would never let anything happen to you, Rimi.*

I put my hands behind my back, and he winds the vine around my wrists. Then we return to the road and join a line of other trolls and orcs waiting to enter the huge city up ahead. They look strangely at us, especially me, the foreign human in their midst. I make a show of pulling away from Lo'zar and trying to make my escape, only for him to roughly yank me back into line. No one seems the wiser.

I take this opportunity to absorb where we are. The trollkin city of Kalishagg is a marvel from afar, with high walls around the outside that would truly make it impossible to invade. It's built onto a hill, so up above the walls I can make out low, rounded buildings that look to be made of clay, and tents of tough leather. In the center, a great tower rising into the air ends in two massive horns, as if it is the head atop the city's body.

When we approach the guards, Lo'zar starts spouting off Trollkin, and again I try to make a run for it to really sell that I'm his prisoner. One of the guards slams down a halberd in front of me and I jump backward. The other one approaches from the side, investigating me curiously. They probably don't see many humans around here.

Lo'zar is still locked in conversation with the other guard, so I ask, *Is everything okay?*

They're trying to get me to pay tax on you.

On me?! It sends a shiver up my spine to think I'm merely transported goods to be taxed. *But you don't have any money.*

While Lo'zar's occupied, the other guard creeps even closer, and sloppily runs a big hand down my body, over my breasts and hip and butt. I jerk away, instinctually drawing into Lo'zar's side. His entire body tenses, and he clenches his fists at his sides—but doesn't move to help. For a moment, the sting of betrayal sweeps through me. He told me he would protect me. The guard gives one last painful pinch to my rear end, but I restrain the urge to smack him away. I can't give them reason to take me from him.

I hope this wasn't all a terrible idea.

That's when Lo'zar reaches for one of his jeweled rings and takes it off. The guards' eyes grow wide, and they readily accept it.

Wait, I say. *That's how you're going to pay?*

Lo'zar doesn't answer as he waits for the guard to hold the ring up to the light, surveying its authenticity. Then he nods and steps aside to let us through, then pockets it.

Surely that was worth much more than me, I tell him.

It was the only way. His expression is intense—furious. *And I would have given him anything to keep you at my side.* He loosens his grip on the vine binding my wrists together. *Now we have to get off the main road so we're not seen.*

We duck into one of the first dark alleyways we find, and before I have a chance to look at our surroundings, Lo'zar lifts me up by the ass and presses me hard against a mortar wall, his lips crashing into mine.

I did not like that, he says, soothing over every inch of my body the guard touched, tenderly caressing it with his familiar hands. *I did not like that at all.* He takes my mouth thoroughly. *I'm so sorry I didn't stop him.*

You couldn't, I say, knowing that as much as it hurt, it's the truth. *Not without giving us away.*

He breathes hard, his forehead resting against mine. *I don't want you to ever doubt how I really feel about you,* he says.

I nod rapidly. *I won't.*

Good. With a quick but bruising kiss, Lo'zar takes my rope and drags me back out of the alley to make a good show of his new prisoner. We start off again down back streets, orcs and trolls alike gaping at me as we pass. A few of them jeer, but no one approaches.

It feels like we walk forever uphill, until Lo'zar abruptly stops in front of a low building. He heads up the steps and I follow tentatively behind as he leads us to a small round door. There, an odd gizmo sits where one might expect a knob or a handle.

Lo'zar fiddles with it, turning one gear to the left, then another gear to the right, and a third gear to the right all the way around. With a *click*, the mechanism releases, and the wooden door is unlocked. He pushes it open and we step inside a small, dim house.

Is this your house? I ask. He shakes his head.

My friend's. Inside, the clay hut is modest, with a fire pit and a few large chairs clearly meant for a trollkin, seated around a small table. Lo'zar leads me to a back room behind a curtain, where the occupant's bed takes up most of the space. He undoes my rope and gestures to the bed.

Why don't you rest for a while? he says. *Graz won't be home anytime soon.*

What about you? I ask. *You've been sleeping on the ground just like I have.*

I'm stronger than you. I feel like I should take this as an insult, but he's right. I wouldn't mind sleeping in the pile of soft furs stacked on the bed.

Okay. I fall into it, allowing myself to be absorbed. Whoever this guy Graz is, I like his idea of relaxing. I'm so exhausted that within moments, the soft furs take me away into darkness.

CHAPTER 17

While Rimi sleeps in the other room, I light a candle and sit down at the fire pit. There's a hole in the roof of the house that lets out the smoke, with a leather tarp strung tight above it so rain can't get in.

I should sleep, but arriving in Kalishagg has sent the blood running too warm in my veins. There are dangers everywhere here, and that guard at the entrance to the city... I curse to myself. If I could have strangled him without revealing our little ploy, I would have. Rimi's terrified face will forever be branded on my memory.

And then there's Graz. I've brought a strange human into his home. I'd like to believe he would have my back, as old friends who grew up street rats together, but clan loyalty is strong, too.

Perhaps it's less about loyalty and more about fear. If Gusak knew I was here, if he thought Graz might be sheltering me...

I don't want to think about that. I have to hope that nobody's seen us yet, and that Graz won't turn us in.

When it grows dark outside, there comes a clicking at the door. Graz is home. I try to appear as non-threatening as I can so I don't surprise him too badly. Finally he comes inside, not even noticing the candle is lit, then turns to close the door behind him.

Graz is certainly no thief. He could walk straight through a herd of elephants and probably not notice them.

"Graz," I say quietly, and he spins around. His eyes land on me with horror.

"Lo'zar?" He takes a few uneasy steps back. After he's recovered a little from his shock, the big orc shakes his head furiously. "That's really you?"

"Who else would I be?"

He groans. "What are you doing in Kalishagg after what you did? Are you a moron?"

I want to skip all this. "Think about it. The fact it's stupid is what makes it brilliant. Gusak isn't looking for me here."

"What if I turn you in?" Graz doesn't sit down, pacing the room instead. "I could hand you over to him easily. I'd probably get a pretty penny for it, too."

"Then do it." I cross my arms. "If my own childhood friend is willing to get me killed, then I deserve it."

Graz stills. When he looks at me again he seems sad and defeated.

"Why would you do this?" he asks. "All... all for a human? You risked everything, Lo'zar. And you're an idiot for coming back."

"You don't understand." I gesture at the chair. "Sit. I have a lot to tell you."

"I don't believe you for a single damn second," my friend says with a measured calmness when I'm finished with my story. I leave out some of the more intimate details, but I don't hide the fact that I'm fucking her. Or whatever it is we do that feels like a lot more than that.

There must be some way to prove it to him. Then I remember the little worms in my pockets, and take them out.

"Here." I hold one out to him. The outer casing is shriveled up, but the body still glows purple. "This is one of the worms we ate."

Silent, Graz takes it and brings it close to his face to study it. He runs a finger along the worm's sinking corpse. "Huh. It looks almost inorganic. Like it's not an animal at all." He stares at me. "So you're saying this stuff inside it... grants wishes?"

"I think so. I wanted to talk to her, and it let me. Except, um, in our minds." Graz stares at me blankly.

"Uh huh." His tone is sarcastic. "Then you ate one to make it permanent. Because that's all very sensible." Graz turns to his bedroom. "And this human you're risking your life for, she's in there?"

I nod. I don't tell him how I feel like I might just wither up and die like that worm when she's gone.

"Maybe if I show you," I suggest. I walk into the other room and kneel down by the bed, giving Rimi's arm a soft shake.

Wake up.

Her eyelids twitch, and then jolt open. Her eyes dart around the room, her pupils dilating like she doesn't remember where we are.

Hey, it's all right. I run a soothing hand over her shoulder. *We're safe—for now. But I need your help.*

She sleepily blinks. *With what?*

First, you should meet my friend. I take her hand and lead her back to where Graz is waiting expectantly. His eyes jump to her, then our linked hands, and the crease between his brows deepens.

"So, this is her?" he asks. "But she's... ugly. I mean, in the way that all humans are ugly. And so *small*."

I have to try hard not to smile. One of the many things I like about her. "I know."

Rimi, I say to her, gesturing at my friend, *this is Graz.*

"Graz," she repeats out loud. She offers him a hand, and Graz looks mighty confused. Then he extends his own hand and they shake, though he rubs it off on his pants afterward.

Graz looks at me. "You can fuck something this size?"

I could strangle him. "Rimi is not a *thing.*"

"Sorry, right. Your human pet."

I growl, and Rimi casts a concerned look between us.

What's he saying? she asks.

He's being rude. I hope against hope that Graz doesn't decide at this moment it's worth more to him to turn us in. *We have to prove to him that my story is true.*

Can I talk to him? she asks. *The way I can talk to you?*

"Hold out the worm," I tell him. "And touch her hand. Then you can—"

"Then I can what, have you both in my head, too?" Graz snorts. "No, thanks. I like my thoughts where they are. Besides, I don't want to overhear whatever gross shit you say to each other."

He won't do it, I tell her.

Rimi pauses to think. Then she grins the grin that says she has an idea. *Let's play a game, then. You go into the other room.*

What? I don't like this already.

Just do it. I'll be okay.

With a reluctant sigh, I agree. I step into the back room, close the curtain, and wait for a few long moments.

I showed him three numbers with my hands, she says through the wall. *Eight, one, and six. Come back now.*

I return to the main room, and hold up the numbers: Eight, one, six.

"This is so fucking strange, Lo'zar," Graz says with a grunt of annoyance.

"I know."

He shakes his head. "There's no way this is real." But I know that he believes it now.

We all sit in silence for a while while Graz processes everything I've told him. He holds up the worm's body to the light.

"So this stuff is dangerous?" he says, examining it closely.

"Dangerous enough we took the whole damn place down with us."

He gapes at me. "You what?"

"Rimi used some of those worms, and they blew up. The pyramid almost collapsed on top of us." Rimi perks up when I say her name. She's glancing between us like she's trying to suss out what we're saying.

I can see the veins already starting to pop out of Graz's forehead. "You... you destroyed one of the few remnants of our ancestors? Before I could even check it out?"

I shrug. "It was that or be killed. I chose 'not be killed'."

He grunts. "I can't believe you. A place filled with some kind of ancient magic, and you just buried it so no one will ever find it again." He shakes his head, then glares at Rimi. "All because you got the hots for a human."

"She's not just any—"

"What do you want from me?" Graz's voice shifts to something harsher.

I swallow hard as I say it. "I need your help getting Rimi home."

This is not what he wanted to hear. "There's no way I'm risking my position with the clan for that," he says firmly, crossing his arms. "I will let you stay here for one night, and then I need you to leave."

My heart falls. I can't do this without my oldest friend to help me.

Rimi notices the atmosphere has changed. *Lo'zar, what's wrong?*

This was my only plan. I don't have any other options. *He won't help us*, I tell her.

She gets to her feet quickly. *Why not?*

You're human. He has no investment in what happens to you. I'm suddenly furious with him. It takes over me hard and fast. This is my person. My everything.

And that's when the truth hits home. Finally, I get it. It all makes sense.

"Graz." I try to keep my temper in check. "I don't think you understand."

"Understand what?" He's just as pissed off with me. "That you put everything on the line for some woman, and now you're bringing that trouble to my house?"

"She's mine," I snarl, locking eyes with him. "She is my mate. Without a doubt. If you turn her away, you are turning me away, forever."

It's like I've shot him right in the gut.

"That's..." Graz is at a loss for words. "That's terrible."

"Terrible?" It's the best thing to ever happen to me. "The mating bond is anything but terrible."

"With a *human?*" He gapes. "It's not possible. And even if it were, it's foolish. Nothing good can come out of it."

Of course something good can come out of it. My happiness. My joy. My completeness.

"Graz." I rise up to my feet, and grip his shoulder in one hand. "Have you ever felt it? What it's like to meet your mate?"

Graz growls at me. "You know I haven't." He drops his head in his hands. "Of course it would be you. The guy who fucks anything with two legs, and does crazy things like stealing from Gusak." I stay silent, letting him get it all out. He looks sad as he turns back to me. "I've always wanted it, you know. A mate. It's not fair that you would find one first."

I think I understand now. "You have plenty of time, Graz." I shake his shoulder. "Maybe you're meant for a little human, too."

"Me?!" He pulls away and groans, looking at Rimi. She returns his stare with an uneasy smile. It's a good thing she can't understand what we're saying. "Never."

I know what it'll take to sell him. I lean forward and whisper in his ear, "They have the tightest cunts you've ever felt in your life."

Then I pull away, and his eyebrows have risen up to his hair. "No way."

"It's the most marvelous feeling in the world. You've never experienced anything like it, I promise."

Rimi's eyes narrow, and I think she might have an idea of what I just said.

"You're serious?" Graz lets out a sigh and runs a hand through his stiff black stripe of hair. "Man, always thinking with your cock, aren't you?"

"It's just one of the many perks."

Graz turns his eyes back to Rimi, and he studies her carefully. "I guess I have no choice." Resigned, he crouches down by the fire pit so he can get a better look at the worm in his hand. "But I don't know how I can possibly help you get her on that ship."

"I know we can figure it out." I grin. "That's what we're good at, right? Finding the impossible path through."

CHAPTER 18

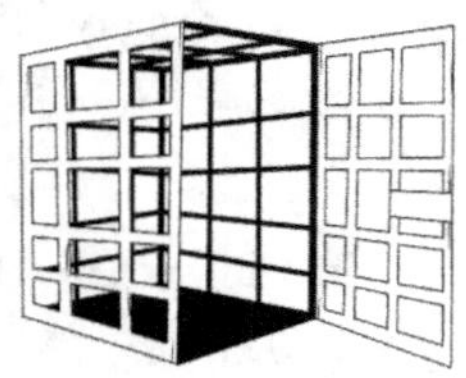

They argue for a long time, Lo'zar and his friend. I try not to look as concerned as I feel. What if this Graz fellow decides to turn us in? Where would we go if he doesn't help us?

But then, it seems like perhaps Lo'zar has gotten through to him. They're discussing something very important, and I wish desperately that I could understand them.

What's going on? I ask as the big orc sits down by the fire and examines one of glow worms.

I think he's going to help us. We'll get you on that boat, Rimi. I promise.

Right. The boat. That's why we're here, after all. Lo'zar risked everything to find me a way home.

I nod slowly. *Okay. I trust you.*

Then, suddenly, the orc sits back on his heels. He turns to Lo'zar, clutching the worm, and talks fast.

What's he saying? I ask.

Something about... Lo'zar trails off as Graz continues gesturing animatedly. *About magic. What else do you know about it?* he asks me. *Are there other legends?*

I try to drag up my memory of all the stories I read as a girl, the history my private tutors taught me.

In the old kingdom, I say, Lo'zar translating, *people had magic. That was how the beast Riggamora grew so strong—by inhaling humans' magic, and that's also why we don't have it anymore.* But maybe we found the remnants of it.

Lo'zar nods quickly and repeats the information to Graz. Then, as if struck by an idea, he suddenly starts gesturing and talking.

What is it? I ask, glancing between them.

Graz has a workshop. Lo'zar's says quickly, like he does when he's excited. *I asked him to see what he can find out about the stuff inside those worms. Maybe turn it into something that could help us.*

I'm flabbergasted. *How?*

He shakes his head. *I don't know. But it worked once, didn't it? Maybe whatever it is, it can help us again.* He looks happy and relieved by this. *If anyone can figure out what it's capable of, it's Graz.*

I find that I don't share his enthusiasm.

Lo'zar

Graz gave me use of his bed with a warning against fucking and ruining his nice blankets. Then he leaves us to experiment with the worms in his shop.

I wonder what my eccentric friend will learn.

After Rimi eats some bread and smoked meat I found in Graz's house, I lead her into the bedroom. I'm ready to get the rest I've been dying for. Bundling her up tightly in my arms, I drape a thick pelt over both of us and wish that I could simply bring Rimi inside myself, where she would always feel at home and never long to be anywhere but with me.

My mate. The one I was born to find. Does she feel it, too? Or am I the only one who's now bound by the rope of fate?

I think about telling her the truth. Maybe then she would stay here. But I have no way of knowing whether she's tied to me as I am to her—if this feeling that she is *mine* belongs only to me.

No. She has to go home, and it would be cruel of me to saddle her with that knowledge.

Lo'zar? Rimi asks, her voice sleepy already. I guess she has a lot of rest to catch up on, too.

Yes?

I'm... I'm scared of leaving you.

All my fondness for her rises up to the top, surging over me like a wave and grinding me into the rocks. That's the very last thing I want for her, to be afraid. *You'll be back where you belong,* I tell her.

Right. She sighs against me, and places a small kiss at the base of my neck. *Where I belong.*

As badly as I want to take her on the floor, I don't. Enjoying her warm body will not help me let her go. But I still hold her tight as we fall asleep.

The next morning before dawn, Graz is shaking me. I blink a few times and find my arm curled tightly around Rimi, who's passed out so cold that there's drool on her lip.

"Get up," he says.

Slowly unwinding myself from my little human, I follow Graz into the main room. Suspicious, he arches an eyebrow.

"You didn't fuck in my bed, right?"

I raise my hands. "Didn't even get a bit of tit."

"Good." He glances through the door to the bedroom. "How did she know all that history stuff?"

"She's not from here." I let out a deep sigh. "She's from the other continent. A place I've never heard of called Yusala."

Graz raises his eyes to mine. "Yusala? That's practically the opposite side of the world, friend."

I suspected as much. It will be a difficult trip, but I will still get her there. "There must be a way."

"Well... I have an idea. Based on what you told me—that you just have to touch it and wish for what you want—I tried it out. It did what you said, and the magic up and vanished on me after I asked it to make Izzy bigger." He holds his arms wide apart. "Damn lizard became five feet long for a minute there."

That doesn't sound very promising.

"But I think I can get around it. I've been thinking how you, uh..." He sticks his tongue out. "How you ate it, and that made it permanent. Maybe if I put it *inside* something, something you could keep close... I haven't figured that out yet. But if you let me use those other worms you found, I will."

I don't have to think twice about it. "You can have them." I pull the other worms from my pocket and this time, Graz gingerly takes them.

"Amazing. This stuff, I've never seen anything like it." His big grin is even wider. "When you're done with your little human there, I want you to show me where this pyramid was. Maybe I can still dig up some of the magic you found at the bottom. You're going to have to leave Kalishagg anyway—Gusak will find you eventually."

"I know." *When I'm done with my little human,* I think sadly.

Lo'zar? It's Rimi's small voice. *When you're done with me?*

Shit. I forgot that I need to control my inner thoughts—and what I broadcast to her. I thought she was asleep.

It was something Graz said, I try to assure her.

I see. She doesn't say anything else after that.

"I need some sleep," Graz grumbles. "Don't go anywhere, okay?"

After he's gone to bed and fallen into a deep slumber, Rimi emerges from the other room and crouches down by the fire, a little distance away from me. Her shoulders are hunched tight.

She hasn't forgotten what I said earlier, and I don't know if telling her that I didn't mean it will work.

Rimi. She twitches a little, but otherwise doesn't acknowledge that I'm talking. *I'm sorry. It's not what it sounded like.* I inhale deeply. I just want to put my arm around her, but I expect she won't take it well now that I've upset her. *I'll never be done with you.* I almost slip up and tell her the truth: that it's impossible. That I'm tied to her now. *You... You mean everything to me, princess.*

The tension in her back softens, just a tiny bit. I crab-walk two steps towards her, and nudge her with my shoulder.

I'm too good of a fuck for that, huh? she asks, and it's both salty and sweet. She doesn't forgive me yet, but she likes me too much to be mad at me.

Right. It's only the fucking that keeps me around. I run a hand down her back, just wanting to touch her, to assure her that she's the only reason my heart is still beating. She leans into me and lets out a sad sigh.

What is it? I ask. *What really upset you?*

I keep thinking about 'after.' I can feel it in my own body when her pulse speeds up. *What will you do after me? And someday, who else will be in your life?* She shivers. *I can't stop thinking about that.*

Who else? I'm mystified by this. *There won't be anyone else.*

Rimi's eyes narrow. *Of course there will be. You're handsome, and funny, and good in bed—*

I cut her off. *No. Don't even say it.* I can't fathom being inside anyone but my princess. I would never be able to bring myself to care the way I care about her. If I did fuck someone else... I would always imagine her, instead.

Lo'zar. Rimi takes my hand and twines her five fingers with my four. *You will have to move on.*

The thought of it is a hot brand burning into my chest. I will never move on. At that moment, I almost tell her—that she's my mate, my everything. She cares about me, I know, but she wants to go home. She *needs* to go home, where she's safe.

So I stop myself and simply hold her hand. I will just have to live the rest of my life feeling what she feels from across the world.

Chapter 19

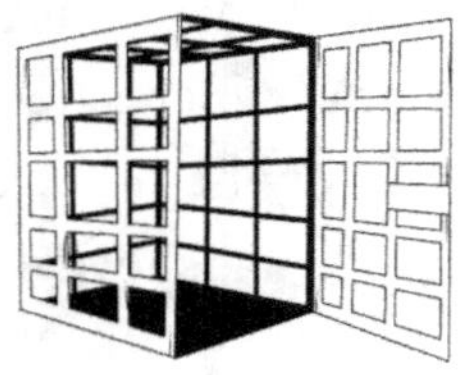

Rimi

My words wounded him, I can tell. But just like he can't live in my world, neither can I live in his. I will only make things harder for him, a human and a trollkin traveling together. He won't be able to stay under his former clan's radar with me clinging to his side, and then he'll have to look after me as well as himself. And who knows what my parents think has become of me? Maybe I've been a burden to them my whole life, but I'd be an even bigger one on Lo'zar.

A little later in the day, I get up to move my body around. I remember what my troll taught me and start the fire. It's not long before he emerges from the bedroom, yawning and stretching. I love his long, lanky limbs, all covered in lean muscle. I remember how they carried me across the jungle, and I love the way they bind me up tight when we're sleeping.

I should get some more food, Lo'zar says. His voice is missing its usual air of confidence. *Graz doesn't have much, and I don't want to eat everything he's got.*

That seems like a bad idea to me, what with his boss's goons out looking for him. *You shouldn't. What if you're caught?*

His grin returns. *You doubt my skills?* he asks playfully. *You clearly didn't meet me as a young thief before I joined the clan. I can move without being seen.*

But I don't like it at all. When he heads to the door to leave, I grab his hand in mine.

Be careful, I tell him. When he looks down at me, I see all the hope and love and tenderness he feels written across his face.

I will. He gives me a squeeze then heads out the door, so I'm left alone in the quiet darkness with nothing to do but put logs on the fire and stew.

When it feels like an hour has gone by, I grow unsettled. Why hasn't he returned yet? I imagine him being kidnapped off the street, dragged back down into those immense caverns, perhaps thrown off the side into the crystal abyss.

I want to go out and look for him, but I know I can't be seen or I'll be apprehended immediately. So I sit and wait, chewing the ends of my fingernails. Just being without him for an hour or two sets me on edge. I want to hear his voice, to feel him near me, to sense that his heart and soul and mind are all close by mine.

Is this what it will be like to be separated?

Lo'zar. I know he will leave a hole inside me, perhaps too big to ever fill.

When I don't hear his footsteps at the front door for another hour, my heart squeezes with panic. What if he needs my help?

So I close my eyes and think as hard as I can: *Lo'zar!*

I don't know if this will work, but I have to try. After a few moments, though, I hear his familiar voice in my mind.

It's all right, princess. I'll be home soon.

When the gadget inside the door clicks, I jump to my feet, worried for a moment it might be one of the clan's goons. But as it opens and I see purple-blue skin in the doorway, I barrel towards him. Lo'zar holds up an armload of food out of the way so I can wrap my arms around his waist and press my face into his chest.

I was so worried, I say. Finally I let him come all the way inside, so nobody sees me.

You were worried about me? He looks quite smug.

Yes, of course. He plops the food down on the table—some bread, meat, and a few vegetables I don't recognize. *When you were gone so long I thought...*

I told you, he chides me, *I am a master thief.*

How did you pay for all this? I ask.

Once again...

You stole it?! I cover my mouth. No wonder he was gone such a long time. Now his grin is even more smug.

Still, you underestimate me. Leaning cheekily against the table, he tears off a piece of bread and holds it out to me. He shakes his head when I reach for it. *Open up.*

I do as I'm told, and Lo'zar slips the food into my waiting mouth. I start to chew, and he looks like he's achieved a great victory. *There. No one can say I don't feed my woman.*

I chuckle as I try to swallow the food, and choke. Lo'zar thumps me on the back. *Too big?* he asks, smirking.

What a demon. I cough a few more times before I have it out of my system. *No,* I say, batting a hand at him. *Just right.*

The smirk fades from his face. He takes a step towards me, and I can clearly see the hunger in his eyes. It's as if he's trained me, because immediately I get warm between the legs. My blood is calling to his, and he answers it, taking my hip roughly in his hand.

He said we couldn't fuck on the bed, Lo'zar says. *That doesn't mean we can't do it somewhere else instead.* He clears the food off the table, and before I can react, he picks me up and sets me on top. Then he unlaces my pants and pulls them off, and I don't argue as he kneels in front of me, face squarely between my knees.

When his mouth is on me, it feels like my blood is racing faster and hotter than my veins can allow. He licks and licks me until I come hard, and once I'm shaking and sensitive, he stands up in front of me. His huge, heavy cock is ready to fill me up, and I want it more than anything.

This time, when he reaches his climax, Lo'zar abruptly pulls out. His seed spills across the table, and he pants hard as the remnants of it drip from his swollen head.

Lo'zar? I ask him, concerned about this change of events.

Just some insurance. He kisses my forehead and holds me against him. But something about it feels ominous in a way I very much don't like.

LO'ZAR

Right when I'm about to shoot everything inside Rimi the way I always do, I remember the captain of the guard—the first human woman I ever fucked—and how she made me pull out right at the end. I thought it peculiar then, because surely a human and a troll can't make whelps. But she seemed concerned enough about it that I did what I was told.

My memory of that moment troubles me so much that I fight my instincts and empty myself on the table, instead.

Damn. Now I'll have to clean it.

Of course, I want nothing more than to see my Rimi all filled up with my seed, dripping from her small hole. I want to see it find purchase inside her, and watch her belly swell up with my whelps. It would bring me the greatest joy possible in this world to lie next to her while she suckles them from her perfect breasts.

But if I'm going to send her home, I can't risk it.

You never seemed worried before, Rimi says, her voice uneasy.

Because before, it didn't feel real that she would leave me. But now Graz is working on a way for her to do just that.

I don't have an answer that will please her, so instead I kiss her and try to distract her with my tongue the way she enjoys. She moans into my mouth and I'm already hard for her again.

Then the lock clicks. I quickly pull up my pants and Rimi does the same. I wipe off my puddle of seed with my shirt just as the door opens. Graz is surprised to see both of us standing there. His eyes narrow.

"Are you doing something gross?" he asks, stomping inside.

"Hardly gross," I answer.

"Filthy." By his face, though, I don't think he's angry. In fact, Graz looks thrilled. "I might have figured something out."

Rimi and I crowd around him as he produces a device. It's a metal box with a chamber inside, filled with glowing violet magic. He holds it up opens the top on a hinge. It reminds me of a music box, but instead of generating a sound, it creates an image.

I peer closer. It's a miniature version of Graz standing atop the box. My friend tweaks something, and the image of him changes. Suddenly he has pale skin, and his hair is ash brown. His tusks vanish. This tiny version of Graz is...

"Human?" I ask, recoiling a little. It disgusts me to see him that way, even if it's only a few inches tall.

He nods feverishly. "Exactly. This is what I would look like, I think, if I were human." He just seems proud of it, and I'm surprised by that, too.

"Disgusting," I say, echoing his sentiment from earlier.

"Indeed. But useful!" He snaps the device shut. "I discovered that if I trap the magic inside this chamber, it won't dissipate when I make a wish. It's like it keeps it in stasis, and the effect stays. I just need a bit more time to get the ask right." He turns to Rimi. "Maybe I could make her look like a trollkin, long enough for her to get on the boat."

What's he saying? Rimi asks. She's still staring at the device. *What was that just now?*

I think he found a way out for you. I try to smile encouragingly. *It will make you look like one of us.*

Oh. Wow. Her eyes are wide. *That's amazing.*

Isn't it? I'm so proud of Graz, and so miserable for myself.

"Thank you, friend," I tell him, clapping him hard on the shoulder. Graz coughs, and then shoves me away.

"Yeah, yeah. As long as it gets you two out of my house, it's worth it. If Gusak found out I was harboring you, he would hang me." But by the tone of his voice, I don't think he really means it.

CHAPTER 20

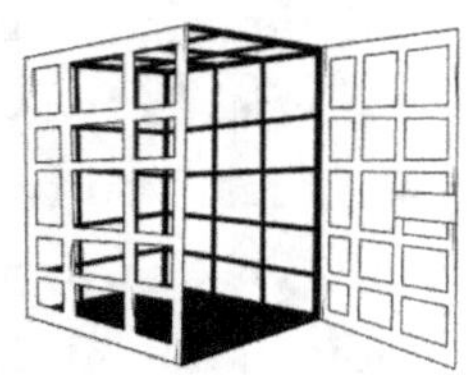

The next day, the air is tense while we wait for Graz to return home. How long do we have until he's finished his device? I am growing tired of sitting around, doing nothing while we wait. The more time passes, the more I find Lo'zar putting up a wall between us. His hand doesn't brush my hip absently as he passes me. He doesn't seek out any excuse to kiss me. There are no wicked or ravishing smiles.

That evening, the door bursts open and it's Graz, and he looks like he's coming out of his skin. He gestures at me to come over, and brings out a device even smaller than before. It hangs from a chain, and he's about to put it on me when Lo'zar stops him.

My troll takes the necklace and gently slides it over my head himself, then lifts up my hair to settle it around my neck.

I don't feel anything change, but Lo'zar and Graz gasp at the same time. When I look down at myself, I find big, blue, four-fingered hands where my pale, five-fingered ones used to be.

You're... Lo'zar's eyes are wide and boggled. *You're a trolless.*

I flex my strange hands, and bring them up to my face. I still feel normal, though.

Graz talks with animation, gesturing while he does.

He designed his wish so it's just an illusion, Lo'zar explains to me. *If someone touches you, they will only find you underneath.*

Got it. Don't let anyone touch me.

He tilts his head at me. *This is very disturbing, I won't lie.*

I shouldn't feel so pleased at the look on his face, knowing that he's only attracted to me and not to the lady troll I look like now. But then I stop my train of thought. No, I want him to be happy when I'm gone. He should be able to find love with someone of his own kind.

I look down at the necklace and run my hands over the odd little device. Now that this is done, we have no excuse to dally any longer. It's time for me to go.

We agree to get on a boat tomorrow. Seeming to sense the solemn air that's fallen on the room, Graz finds his way to his bed in the corner and says goodnight to us. We both thank him profusely, but he just waves us off.

He's keeping the rest of the worms for himself, Lo'zar explains.

What's he going to do with them?

Lo'zar shrugs. *Hell if I know.*

Once we're inside the bedroom, Lo'zar hastily takes the necklace off of me. He breathes a sigh of relief when I'm back to myself again, and his hands travel from my cheeks down to my hips, as if he's reminding himself what I really look like. Then he pulls me roughly against him.

Lo'zar? I ask. But he doesn't say anything, just holds me hard and fast, as if he'll never let me go. Still wrapped around me, he falls to the bed, and soon his hands are underneath my shirt, tracing every last inch of me. His touch is almost feverish, and his mouth descends on mine with a ravenous hunger.

I thought Graz asked us not to—

I don't care. Lo'zar's voice is surprisingly harsh. *I want you. And I want you now.*

I don't object as he takes off my shirt and lavishes attention on my nipples. He plays with them harder than he ever has before, and I cringe under his hands. What's gotten into my troll? Something about my strange transformation has unsettled him. He's turned hard and serious, very unlike Lo'zar. When he kisses me, he nibbles my lips so forcefully that his sharp canines leave marks, and when his hand ducks into my pants, he finds my entrance and pushes a finger into me, even though I'm not very wet yet.

Please, I ask him quietly. *Be gentle.*

He freezes, and then he pulls his arm back harshly. His head drops to my chest, and when I touch his cheek, he's trembling all over.

Lo'zar? I ask, growing concerned. While I run my hands through his hair, he buries his face deeper into me, like he wants to do anything but look at me.

I'm sorry, he says with nothing but misery in his voice. *I'm so sorry.*

It's okay. Wrapping my arms around him, I lean down to kiss his head. *What's wrong?*

Everything. But he doesn't say more, and this time when he holds me, his arms are sweet and soft and loving. As he nuzzles my neck, he breathes in deeply, like he's taking in the smell of me as much as he can. I hold him close, wishing I could make all of his pain go away, even though I'm the cause of it.

Lo'zar, I say, lifting his head. *Will you be here with me? Please? While we still can?*

He clutches me tight against himself. *Always,* he says. *I will always be here with you.*

His hands cover every inch of my body, tenderly cupping my soft curves, tasting me with just the tips of his fingers. Lo'zar's breathing speeds up as I mold into his touch, letting myself fall into him. This time when he samples my breasts, he's velvety and sensual. He scoots down so he can brush his tongue across each nipple, savoring them slowly, pausing to rest his forehead between them.

My princess, he says, and it's not in his usual teasing tone. He kisses from my collar down my belly, pausing at the gap between my oversized pants and my hips. He slides my clothes down slowly, his lips trailing over each bit of exposed skin, until he has my legs up in his arms while he kisses my calf, my ankle, my toes. Then he returns to the soft place between my thighs and breathes gently on it.

Your scent is perfect, he says reverently, closing his eyes. *I could just drink you in forever.*

I consider cracking a joke about how disappointing that would be, but I keep quiet, because for once there is nothing joking about Lo'zar's expression. He brushes his tongue over my clit, just a feather touch, and I squirm underneath him. I know I can't make a sound—Graz forbade us from doing this in his bed. I feel guilty, but I want nothing more than my troll on top of me, inside of me, surrounding me. I need to remember him.

He repeats the motion again, and I sink into the soft furs, luxuriating in his touch. My eyes fall closed and my head drifts back as his delicious mouth speeds up, giving me the last push I need to crack open, and then I'm spilling out, all my wishes and fears.

As my body seizes, I slap a hand over my mouth to hold in the sound. Lo'zar slides back up my body, licking his lips, until our hips are pressed together and his heavy cock is squashed between my thighs, the shaft rubbing over my most tender place. He sighs into my ear as I rock against him, desiring him with all of myself.

Lo'zar, I say, brushing back some of his wild hair. *Please. I want you. Right now.*

His orange eyes lock with mine, and in them I can see everything: his hope, his longing, his pain. Every last one of my emotions is reflected back at me, and all I want is to hold him close to me forever, the weight of his body on mine holding me to the earth.

He doesn't need to look down as he spreads my legs, hooking my knees over his hips, because our bodies already know just how to join together like pieces of a puzzle. No, he remains staring into me, watching every movement of my face as he brings his soft cockhead to the smooth, slick cavern where it belongs. It slips between my edges, fitting perfectly inside me. I try my hardest not to make a sound as he delves in only an inch, then retreats, letting me shift and conform to his shape. Then another inch, and another, as his swollen cock spreads me wide for him. When it seems like I won't be able to hold in my moans any longer he kisses me, swallowing my desperate sounds into his own mouth.

I will always be with you, he says, cupping my face in one hand as he continues his progress deeper and deeper inside me. *Even when we're apart, you will be the first thing on my mind when I wake up every day, and the last thought I have when I go to sleep.*

My face aches with unspent tears as he tells me these words, because I know I will always feel the same way.

"Lo'zar," I whisper to him as he finally sinks the rest of the way in, and he lets out a shuddering breath. There are so many words I want to say, things hiding just inside my lips, but that would only hurt more. I will remember him as long as I live, and even afterwards. I know I'll never find again what I've found here, wrapped up in him—my cocky, handsome, big-hearted troll.

I press my face into his neck to stifle the tears as he gently moves inside me, one slow, agonizing stroke at a time, swirling up the small strands of my pleasure into a big, glowing ball of bliss. My legs wrap tight around his waist as his mouth grows more urgent against mine. I feel it in my own heart as the beat of his quickens, as his blood moves faster and faster, hot and filled with need. I hear his thoughts in mine, all his affection and joy and misery scrambled in one wild orchestra.

I don't know how long we make love like this, tangled in each other, memorizing every last crease and swell of each other's bodies, but I never want it to end. I have to shove blankets into my mouth to silence myself, but Lo'zar's grunts are almost as loud.

I can't wait to feel you come around me, he says, his mental voice unsteady with emotion. *I want to feel all of you, my sweet, lovely, perfect princess.*

I obey. My body clamps down tight, and a cry surges from my mouth into the blankets. The pleasure sweeps over me, meeting a tidal wave of heartbreak on the other side. Tears finally break free as he yanks his cock out of me, and spills his generous seed between my thighs, instead. It makes me feel so empty, so hollow inside, that my tears morph into sobs, and I bury my face in the bed in an effort to be quiet.

Rimi? he asks with concern. I just shake my head, unable to stop the flow, or even to say a single word. His arms pull me in tight, gripping me like iron, and he buries his face in my neck as I cry. I feel his own wet tears on my skin, and the last piece of me breaks.

We lie like that until there's nothing left inside either of us. Two husks, we eventually fall asleep into a shared dream where all of this is different.

CHAPTER 21

Lo'zar

The idea that she'll leave me finally became real when I saw her transform from my delicate Rimi to a big, tall trolless, one who would easily fit in anywhere in Kalishagg, anywhere in trollkin lands. Now there should be no problem with getting her aboard the ship.

I was desperate to keep her, but she is not a thing to be kept. She deserves her home in the stars.

When we wake up the next morning, it's time to go.

"Thank you, friend." I clap Graz on the back, but I don't feel the words. I almost wish that he'd failed, even though I know a gifted mind like his would never be outsmarted, even by magic. "I'm sorry for being a pain in your ass."

Graz shrugs. "Yeah, you were. But I'm going to make good use of that stuff you brought me." He wags a finger. "You're going with her, aren't you?"

"Just until Eyra Cove," I say.

He sighs. "Then draw me a map, at least, of where you found

that stuff."

"You don't need one. You already found it. It's on that map in your shop."

Graz's eyes widen. "Why didn't you say anything? So I was right. Those books I found…" He trails off. "Well, if you're headed to the cove, you should know that the necklace will work on you, too." He eyes me. "In case you need to pass as human for a while."

Me, looking like a human? Blegh.

He hands me a copy of the boat schedule, then gives a little wave at Rimi. "She's actually not so bad," he admits as he steps out the door. "I think I can tell what you see in her, Lo'zar." Graz looks uncertain, and his voice drops low. "Are you sure you want to send her home if she is who you think she is? What will happen to you?"

I knows what he means: the torture of being separated. But I don't have a choice. "There's no life for her here," I say.

"What about a neutral city?" he asks. "Go to the desert. Gusak would never follow you there."

I shake my head. "She wants to return to her family. Besides," I shrug, "like you said, she's human. It would never work."

Graz nods in understanding, though there's a shred of pity in his eyes.

"Sorry it turned out this way," he says. "Maybe I'll see you again someday."

And then he's gone.

Rimi doesn't have any things to pack, so I fill up a couple bags of food to bring along on the trip. I'll be taking her as far as I can since she doesn't know the way. We'll ride a trollkin boat to Eyra Cove, a neutral city in an island chain, where she'll take off her necklace and transfer to a human ship, one that should be able to get her home—or most of the way, at least.

Our plan is to wait until the last moment, before the ship is set to take sail, and get aboard before any of Gusak's goons have the opportunity to catch us. When we're ready to go, Rimi slips on the necklace and changes right in front of me.

Her troll form is almost as tall as I am, with a shock of purple hair and pale blue skin. The only hint that she isn't truly troll is her eyes, which remain the same human shape and color as her own.

Then we're off. We keep to shadows, side roads and alleyways as we move through Kalishagg toward the dock. I tie a bandana around my head to cover my hair, and switch into some of Graz's dirty machinist clothes to blend in. I even smudge grease on my face hoping we can make it onto the boat before anyone recognizes me.

Finally, in the distance I can make out the tall masts of ships at the dock. We'll have to be out in the open to reach the boarding ramp, but if we can make it quick, our chances seem as good as when we entered the city a week ago. I have the coin ready to go— Graz went and sold one of my gold chain necklaces for it. I'd picked it right off an old trolless's neck. Now I'm down to two rings and one necklace, the last of my coin without the chest I left under my bunk. I only started collecting them as a reminder of where I came from, and a promise that I'd never end up there again.

But none of that matters now. It's enough to get Rimi where she's going, and then take me somewhere I don't have to keep looking over my shoulder for Gusak's men.

As the time approaches, I take Rimi's hand in mine. She's quivering, her eyes following every trollkin passerby like she's expecting someone to sniff her out. Squeezing her fingers in mine, I'm reminded of when she was trapped inside her cage and I passed her food through the bars, then held her hand like this.

I'm sorry I keep putting you in danger, Rimi says, as if she can read my mind. *First you saved me, and now you're helping me get home, all at your own expense.*

I shake my head furiously. *Freeing you was the best decision I've ever made.*

At last, an orc at the top of the ship ramp shouts, "Final boarding call!" That's our cue. Tugging Rimi's hand, we step out of the shadows together, just two trolls getting on a boat out of here. We make our way across the busy platform, dodging other trollkin as we go. The ramp is just ahead—only a few more feet to go before we're home free.

A heavy hand lands on my shoulder, and I freeze.

"I have to give you props." It's Kugara's voice. When I turn to look over my shoulder, she and two of Gusak's other goons have already started to circle us, their weapons drawn. "Clever move, coming back here."

Shit. I let go of Rimi's hand. *You need to run.*

Run?! Her eyes flick to Kugara and then back. *I'm not leaving you, Lo'zar.*

You have to. Please.

But she doesn't listen. No, she stands by my side, as if she's ready to fight with me. Damn it, my brave princess. She'll get herself killed before she can go back home.

The first of Kugara's blows lands on my cheekbone, sending me reeling back. The other smashes into my gut, but she's not strong enough to knock me too far off balance. My reflexes are lightning quick, too, and soon I've got my gun out in one hand, my sword in the other. One of the goons, a guy who's face I recognize but name I don't remember, joins the fray. I slash him with the sword, twisting my body around to keep Rimi behind me, and the grunt cries out as I drag the blade across his front.

Once more Kugara tries to hit me, but I duck under her hand. "You shouldn't have left your little hideout," she says. "Some of Gusak's eyes saw you. We've been waiting a while for you to show up."

While she's busy talking, I jam the butt of my gun into her chest. She stumbles back. "Three-to-one?" I ask, sneering, as the third goon approaches armed with a gun of his own.

Rimi, please, I tell her, as I swing my sword and it smashes into the barrel of the gun. *Please run.*

I won't! Suddenly, she leaps out from behind me, tackling the second goon, who was apparently coming in hot with an axe in one hand. Though she doesn't knock him over, she takes him enough by surprise that he stumbles backward. I would've been cleaved right through the brain if she hadn't saved me just then.

Kugara recovers quickly, but I'm already crouching low to the ground, swinging one leg out wide to slam into hers. Her knees give and she falls down, and suddenly I have my gun to her head. The other two grunts freeze.

"Let us go," I say calmly, "or I blow her brains out."

"Fine," one of them says, and he raises his own gun. "Do it." But I'm much faster, and I turn the barrel from Kugara's temple to his face, where I press the trigger. The shot goes right through his head, and I hear Rimi gasp in surprise as blood splatters all of us. Before anyone can react, I lunge at the other grunt with my sword, burying it deep in his chest.

Kugara is still on her knees, covered in the blood of her two compatriots. She holds up both hands in surrender.

"Lo'zar," she says quietly. "Please don't kill me. I was just obeying Gusak's orders."

Guards are already starting to push their way through the crowd that's gathered around our fight. "I won't kill you," I tell her. "This time." I holster my gun, then my sword. "Oh, and tell Gusak not to bother. He'll never find me." With that, I grab Rimi's hand.

Now we run, I say, and we take off at a sprint toward the boat. They're starting to wind up the ramp, so I pick her up under my arm and leap, landing just on the edge of it. My balance sways, so I toss her forward, and the motion sends me sprawling onto the ship's deck. Down below, guards are shouting and waving their weapons.

The orc in charge of boarding has his arms crossed as he examines us.

"You'd better have the coin for all this ruckus," he tells me as the boat starts to move. Guards are streaming down the dock, but it's too late. "I can stop the ship and hand you over."

"Don't worry." I pull out my bag and drop twice as much as our fare into his hands. I'll still have plenty for the rest of our trip. "Thanks."

He sighs and gestures for us to enter the cabin.

We made it. The time has come.

Chapter 22

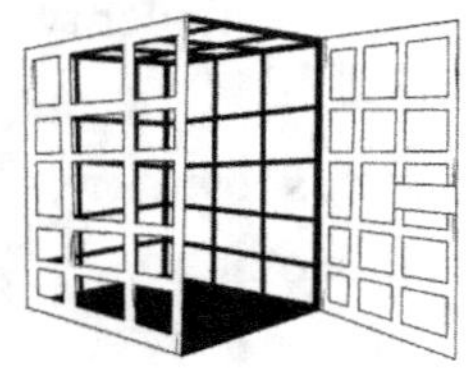

RIMI

I know after his fight on the dock that Lo'zar can protect me from anything. That he *will* protect me, at any cost to himself, and it hurts to know this and still be leaving him.

Our journey is, thankfully, an uneventful one. We share one tiny bed in the cabin of the ship, snuggled tight together so our limbs don't fall off the side. I keep my amulet on me at all times, only turning it on when I need to leave the room. I don't talk, because my voice would give me away.

At night my troll holds me close, and sometimes when the dark and the quiet and our own heartbeats are too much, he reaches down between my legs to touch me, swirling his finger around until I'm panting and wet. Then he slides into me from behind, filling me up as far as he can, and gently stroking in and out until I'm up in the clouds and floating away, forgetting about what waits for us on the other end of this trip. We both bury our misery in each other's bodies, desperation in our every movement, trying to quiet the pain with pleasure, but it only makes my heart ache worse.

He always pulls himself out at the last moment and unloads onto the bed. It makes me feel strangely empty inside.

Lo'zar talks to fill the hours, and I close my eyes and listen to the sound of his voice in my head. He tells me about his childhood growing up on the streets, stealing what he needed in order to eat and living in dark alleyways, always ready to defend himself. My life has been filled with privilege, I realize. Never once did I worry about where my next meal would come from. I try to commit his voice to memory as he tells me how the clan found him, and Gusak took him in.

He exploited you, I tell him. *You were desperate and young, and he knew what to say to bring you to heel.*

I was a ruffian. I needed to be brought to heel.

I shake my head. *What you needed was love, and food, and shelter.*

His smile is like smooth chocolate. *You have such a big heart,* he says, running his fingers over my knuckles. *How do you have so much love to give?*

My parents never gave me any, so what was the point in giving them love in return? I push some wild hair away from his face. *I saved it all up for you.*

He brings me in close, folding himself around me like I'm about to vanish. He buries his face in my neck and says nothing, but I can feel the heaving of his chest.

It's too soon when we reach Eyra Cove, a neutral city that operates as a port for trollkin and humans alike. This is where we are supposed to part ways. Certainly a human ship here will be bound for the other continent.

When we get off the boat, I'm struck by the strangeness of this city, where human and trollkin alike do business side-by-side, even bartering and trading with one another. Suddenly I'm much less sure of myself, of what I'm doing. Could Lo'zar and I simply stay here and blend in?

But Lo'zar is anxious the moment we step on dry land, worried that Gusak has expanded his operation here, too. He keeps a close watch while I take off my amulet and start inquiring at different ships about their destinations. When I mention Yusala, each of the boat masters shakes their head. "We don't travel to the other continent," they all say. "You'll have to wait for the big ship."

I don't know what they mean by *the big ship*, but we take up a room at the local inn, and every day we check from our window to see if it's arrived. Only a few days later, the gargantuan ship docks.

It has three full masts, clearly designed for long ocean voyages. I swallow hard.

It's your way home, Lo'zar says.

Of course, I nod and agree, trying to seem happy that the moment is here—but inside all I feel is dread. *I know it will be a long trip, but will you go with me?* I take his hand in mine and weave our fingers together. *I'm afraid.* Actually, I'm terrified of being alone on that boat without him.

His lips tug up at the side, and he nods his head. *Of course.*

Even if it means wearing the amulet? I ask.

Even then.

Lo'zar doesn't have a lot of coin left, but it's enough. The afternoon of our departure, he puts on the amulet and flicks the switch. All at once, he transforms. And even though it's just an illusion, I'm terrified by what I see.

As a human, his skin is a medium brown, and he has wild blond hair like he was bathed in sunlight from an early age. His eyes remain the same, though—orange and lively, just like my troll.

Hmm. It is very disconcerting, I tell him. *I see what you mean now.* I don't like this version of him, but at least his internal voice still sounds like himself.

When we board the ship together I can feel the end drawing nearer, and my hope that something will stop this starts to die.

LO'ZAR

It is unnerving to look down and find a five-fingered human hand. I don't like wearing the amulet, but if this is what it takes to be near Rimi for just a while longer, I'll do it—even if it means another long voyage across the sea and back again.

I don't know what I'll do after. I have to find somewhere to go where the tendrils of Gusak's power can't reach me. I'll miss the life of organized crime, but anything above pickpocketing is a dead-end for me now.

We spend more time in the quiet, both of us tense and steadily drawing inward. One evening, she starts to tap her finger impatiently, and I join her, making a little rhythm between our hands. At first, she's pleased, and we create a symphony of percussion between us. But soon her eyes grow sad and she slows down, until we're both back to keeping our hands clutched tight at our sides.

It feels like both forever, and no time at all, when we finally arrive at our destination.

We're standing at the top of the ramp, other human passengers pushing past us, when I realize I can't possibly let her go. Not yet. I just need a little more time with my clever, perfect girl, even if it means surrounding myself with humans in this bustling port town.

We walk down the ramp together, and she gives me a questioning look at the bottom.

I want to make sure you get there safely, I tell her.

She tilts her head, studying me curiously, then nods. *All right.*

Thank you. All of our conversations have become like this: stilted and formal.

Using my last few coins, Rimi finds a carriage that will take us to her home in the countryside. Everything is so very different here, from the brick architecture to the golden trees to the smell of lavender in the air. It's almost pleasant being somewhere so clean, so neat, every edge tidily tucked in. I have never seen a place this alien, and yet it's beautiful. No wonder she came from here—it's just as otherworldly as she is.

The carriage takes us across even more lovely landscape, through valleys and meadows, and over quaint wooden bridges with burbling brooks passing underneath. Even as I enjoy this mysterious place, now the moment is coming when I finally won't have a choice but to say goodbye.

When we arrive, it is like some sort of palace, gargantuan and sprawling and painted a prim white, with green hedges around the outside acting as a wall to the world. The sky is a perfect blue, spotted with a handful of clouds. Everything is quiet save for the occasional chirping of a bird.

So this is where Rimi grew up. Suddenly I understand a good deal more about her.

My home, she says, as the carriage comes to a stop. She climbs out, and I'm about to follow her, when I realize that I have nothing left to say or do.

There's a questioning look in her eyes when I don't exit the carriage with her.

Lo'zar? she says, fear creeping into her voice.

This is your stop, I tell her, and try my hardest to smile while everything inside me shatters to pieces.

But what about you? Her hands clench together tight.

I'm going home, I say. *We both knew that.*

Right.

The driver of the carriage looks annoyed that we're taking so long, nothing but silence between us. *You should go*, I say.

But she doesn't turn to walk away, not yet. *I'm so glad I met you, Lo'zar.* Those familiar silver-gray eyes find mine, and when she looks at me, she *sees* me. I know then she can feel the bond between us, too. Maybe she doesn't have a name for it, but she understands that we will both be torn in half.

I'm glad I met you, too, Rimi. Her name hangs in the space between us. Her last smile is like a rare piece of art, one that I would steal and hoard next to my bed for the rest of my life.

With that, she turns around and starts towards the house, down the neatly-trimmed pathway. When the driver rouses the horses, I stop him with one hand and shoot him a deadly look. He seems to register that there's something not right about me—I'm going to guess it's the eyes—and so he obeys, dropping the reins.

I watch and watch until Rimi reaches the house, where she stops to knock on the door. I'm not breathing as she waits, and then, the door opens.

With a sharp exhale, I turn away and gesture at the driver that it's time to go. He's irritated with me, but doesn't try to talk as the horses start up into a trot and we leave the house behind.

I feel like I've made the biggest mistake of my life. But some mistakes have to be made for us to learn and grow, don't they? I will never fall for a human again. Or anyone, for that matter. I know that someday, when my Rimi dies, I'll die along with her. A mated soul cannot exist alone.

Maybe when that time comes, I'll get to see her again.

The carriage carries me farther and farther from her, until we're crossing the brook and heading down into the valley, toward the port town that will take me far away from here and back to my own world.

Chapter 23

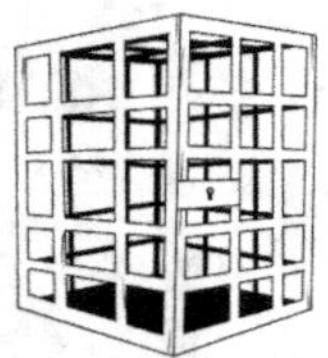

It's our servant, Ania, who answers the door. If I were in a laughing mood, the look on her face would send me into a fit. But all I can think about as she takes me in, sputtering with disbelief, is what I felt when Lo'zar told me he was glad to have met me.

Together. We're supposed to be *together*. In that moment it was the only thing in the world I knew for certain.

But we've already decided. This is what's best for both of us.

After she's gotten over her shock, Ania hugs me tight and then pulls me inside the house, screeching my name up the stairs. Everything around me is familiar—the carved wood furniture, the vases of flowers, the paintings hanging on the walls—but it's like I'm wading through a dream, where it's not quite all real.

This place doesn't know who I am anymore.

I hear thumping along the second floor, and my mother appears at the top of stairs in a whirlwind. Her eyes are wide and surprised, but she is not smiling.

"Rimi?" She slowly comes down, like she doesn't believe I'm standing in front of her. Her sharp features are the same as when I left, and her eyes just as critical. "Is that really you, Rimi?"

"Who else?" I try to smile, to show my mother I'm glad to see her again, but it feels flat on my face.

"I'm going to find the master," says Ania, running off into the house. "He won't believe it!"

My mother marches down the steps one at a time until she's in front of me. She takes my elbow in her hand, just like she always does when she's about to chastise me for something. What could I have done wrong?

"How did you get here?" she asks.

"It was a long trip, I'll tell you that." I wonder what she thought happened to me when I vanished in the middle of the night. "Whoever kidnapped me, they took me really far away. I went through a lot to get home, Mother."

Her hand tightens on my elbow. "Why? Why would you do that?"

She's behaving so strangely. I'm her daughter, after all. This is my home. Of course I would do whatever was in my power to come back.

"Because I love you." I've never said it before, and neither have they—but I wouldn't have gotten on that ship if I didn't know my parents were mourning me.

My mother doesn't say anything to that as she starts to lead me down the hallway by the arm. "Well, I'm glad you did, honey," she says, a little more sweetly than I expect from her. "Because now we can fix what went wrong."

Does she mean... with us? Between her and me and my father? If I have to live a life apart from Lo'zar, then I would hope it's a happy one, where I can have a loving family.

"Great," I say. I'm not sure where she's taking me, though. We walk through the kitchens, to the low door that leads into the cellar. She unbolts it. "Are we getting some wine?" I ask. Perhaps we're celebrating my return.

"Yes." I follow her down the steps into the darkness. She gestures at the room. "Please, pick out something."

While I'm looking through the bottles, I hear her footsteps head back up the stairs. I turn around. "Mother?"

The door slams. The bolt locks.

I run up the steps, my blood thundering past my ears. No. I can't be locked in. I can't be trapped here.

I will not live in a cage again.

"Mother?" I call out, trying not to panic even though my hands are already shaking, even though I can feel the iron bars around me and see the holes in the crate over my head. "Mother?!"

"We won't make the same mistake twice," her voice says through the door. "Those idiot trollkin couldn't be trusted. The buyer will come and collect you personally this time."

"The buyer?" I repeat, rather stupidly, because it's now perfectly obvious to me what I missed all along.

No one kidnapped me from my bed.

I was sold—probably to pay off my parents' debts. By coming home, all I've done is put myself back in a cage.

A terrible rage comes over me. I scream and bash the door with my fist. I will not be locked up, not again, to be sent across the ocean in a barrel. I hit the door, over and over, until my screams come out hoarse.

Nobody comes.

Lo'zar, I think. Tears roll down my face in hot waves. My pulse is going so fast I feel like I might tip over and pass out. *Please. Come back. Please help me!*

LO'ZAR

Lo'zar. It's Rimi's voice, but it's faded. Muffled. It cuts out, and then returns again. *...Help me!*

Rimi?! I stand up in the carriage, surprising the driver and the horses. I call out as loud as I can into our shared mental world. *Rimi! What's wrong?!*

Help! is all I hear back. I can feel that she's desperate, gasping for air.

I grab the carriage driver by the shoulder, and frantically I gesture back the way we came, because I have to return to the house behind the hedges. Rimi is in trouble. When she walked up to that front door, I knew something was wrong. Leaving her there flew in the face of every instinct I have. I should have listened to myself.

The carriage driver doesn't want to obey me, and I don't have the words to demand it, so I slide off one of my rings. I took that one when I spotted it through a window, and the jewel reminded me of a crescent moon. I push it in his face and point back the way we came.

The man hastily snatches the ring, shoves it in his pocket, and wheels the horses around until we're riding back toward where I never should've left Rimi in the first place. We gallop and gallop down the pebble road, until the house appears in my vision again.

Rimi! I call out.

Lo'zar?!

The moment we reach the front drive I'm vaulting out of the carriage. I hold up my hand to the driver, telling him to wait, and he drops the reins. He won't go anywhere, not while I still have more rings on my fingers.

Where are you? I ask her, heading towards the front doors. I yank off the necklace, ready to wreak havoc, and bowl them open.

A woman in an apron screams when she sees me, a huge, angry troll charging into her living room.

I'm in the cellar! Rimi cries desperately.

What's a cellar?

Go to the back of the house! My parents, they— She breaks off, and I can feel the terror in her heart.

I'll find you. I rampage down the hallways, knocking over tiny human furniture that gets in my way. Where is the back of the house? The woman behind me is still screaming, and I nearly bowl over two more humans as I enter what looks like a big, fancy kitchen, the air smelling of rich food.

There's a door, Rimi whispers. *A small wooden door.* I look around for it, while the humans yell and flee. There.

I race over and try the handle, but it appears to be bolted. Instead, I yank as hard as I can and the door simply comes off its hinges. I throw it to one side.

There, huddling in the darkness, is my Rimi.

I pick her up in one swoop. Her face is red with tears and her eyes wide and wild.

I'm here, I say, crushing her to my chest. She grabs my tunic and sobs into it. *I'm here.*

They... They... She gasps with the crushing power of her misery. *I wasn't taken, Lo'zar. They sold me.*

A violent, searing fury rips through me. Her family sold their only child? I should kill them.

Where are they? I demand. *How could anyone do this?*

I don't know. She looks up at me with those eyes that can see right to the core of me. *Please, can we... can we get out of here?*

I'll destroy them, I think to her, hard. *I will end them for what they've done to you.*

She shakes her head furiously. *No. I want to go. I want to leave this place and never look back.*

As much as I desire revenge, she doesn't want that. She wants to be free, and I understand that feeling more than any other.

Holding her to my hip with her legs wrapped around my waist, I turn back the way I came, sprinting at my full speed. When we reach the main room, the sound of a gun deafens me.

A man is shouting something behind us. I turn around, right as another shot rings out. A searing agony tears through my arm, and I almost drop Rimi. There's a man in strange, fine clothes holding a long gun I've never seen before.

He yells at me, but I can't understand it. I don't need to. I lunge towards him, grabbing the barrel of the gun in my hand just as he fires it again. The shot flies over my shoulder, into a chandelier high up overhead. I twist the barrel, with all the strength I have in my injured arm, and the gun snaps. The man's eyes are huge and terrified as I tower over him, hurling the gun off to one side. I could kill him right now without much extra effort.

He turned his own child over to monsters for a profit, to be used how they saw fit.

Father! Rimi reaches for him. *Please, Lo'zar! Don't do it.*

My fury ebbs just a little, and I shove the man hard, knocking him down. Then I turn away and my long legs carry us out the front door, into the sunshine.

The carriage is still waiting. I sprint back, holding Rimi with my good arm, and jump inside. The driver is wide-eyed.

Tell him to go, I say. *Tell him to take us back to the ship.*

Rimi says something to the man as I set her down in the carriage next to me, and soon we're galloping away, leaving this terrible place behind.

CHAPTER 24

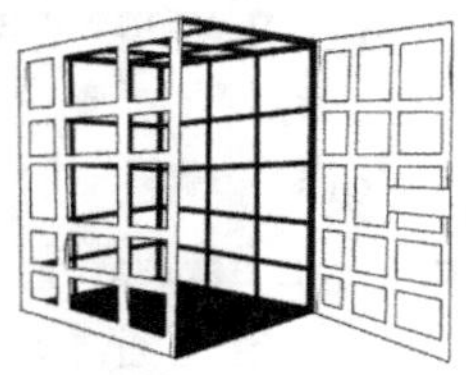

RIMI

I'm still in shock when we reach the city. It doesn't make sense that my parents could have seen me as currency, an object to be sold to the highest bidder. Love was scarce in our home, but that didn't mean I was disposable.

And now, I have nothing left. Nothing but my troll.

Lo'zar holds me close to his side, his illusion restored, even though his arm is bleeding. The driver squeezes himself into the corner as far as he can and doesn't speak to us, and once he deposits us at our destination, he seems immensely grateful to be rid of us.

We have to sell Lo'zar's last ring for enough coin for both of us to return on the ship, which hasn't departed yet. It will leave in the morning, once the rest of the passengers have arrived. I buy a few medical supplies so I can treat the shallow wound on his arm, and we board.

Once we're safe in our cabin, I start to break apart. I shed every last tear left in my body, trying to wash off the sting of betrayal. My home, my family, everything I've ever known is gone.

Lo'zar just holds me as the sobs wrack my body. When there's nothing left, I curl up at his side.

I'm sorry, is all he says.

⁂

I have a long time to recover on our journey. I don't want to talk about my old life—all I want is to imagine my new one, where I could go now that I know there's nothing holding me back.

They're dead to me.

Where can we possibly go? I ask Lo'zar. *Where Gusak won't be looking for you?*

He sighs. *I don't know. As we saw in Kalishagg, he has eyes everywhere.* The only place we've been safe has been out on the open ocean.

Whatever we do, we have to be able to survive. Make a living. I have no skills, no knowledge, no craftsmanship. At least Lo'zar can steal to get by, but I'm not a sneak thief. I'm just a drain.

Hey. Lo'zar captures my chin in his hand, and leans down to peck me on the lips. It feels good and familiar and right. *We can figure this out. I'll do whatever I have to do to take care of you.*

But what about you? I ask. *Who will take care of you?*

A mischievous twinkle flashes in his eyes. *I am an easy beast,* he says. *Sit on my cock every night and I will be plenty happy, no matter where we are.*

I whack him on the shoulder, and he just lets out a belly laugh.

Be serious for a moment.

Lo'zar sighs and leans back on the bed, running his hand through my hair absently. *Well, I am quite serious about that,* he says. *But I don't have any trades either, Rimi. Well, except the one you already know about. And that's not quite an honest living.*

Honest? I laugh. *No one asked about honest.*

His eyebrows jump, and then that familiar wide, boyish grin spreads across his face.

In that case, he says, *we could stop in Eyra Cove and see what... less savory elements might be there.*

And serve another big boss? I ask. *That's not you, Lo'zar. You should be a free agent.* My troll is clever and smart. He doesn't need someone else telling him what to do.

He thinks about this for a long moment.

A free agent. A pair of free agents.

I nod in agreement. *Teach me your ways, master.*

He chuckles and pushes a lock of hair behind my ear. *I'll teach you everything I can.* The longer he looks at me, the more his expression becomes soft and full of something I don't quite recognize.

Rimi, he says. *Have you felt it?*

I'm confused by the subject change. *Felt what?*

The bond between us. His hands trail down my arms to my sides, over my hips, then back up to my heart. *The feeling you can't shake like this was supposed to happen. Like we were meant to find each other.*

Oh. That feeling. *Yes. I know it well.*

His grin widens when I say it as if it's the most obvious thing in the world. He slides towards me on the bed, drawing me into his lap, where his eyes bore into mine.

You're my purpose, Rimi. My everything. My mate. And I'll do whatever I have to do to give you the life you deserve with me.

I tilt my head. *Your mate? What's that?* My brain doesn't seem to recognize the word that he's using.

It means you're stuck with me. Forever.

Oh. I lean into his side and inhale the familiar smell of him, like that first blanket he gave me. It smells of sunshine, of home—my real home, now. *That's fine.*

'Fine'? he asks with a snort.

More than fine. Good. Very good.

You don't know about the other part of it, he says. His cock is already thick and warm under his breeches, and it presses into my thigh with some urgency.

The other part? I ask as he takes off my shirt, and then his own. He starts to cover me in kisses, from my throat to my belly.

About being mates. He sucks on each of my nipples, meaningfully. *I'm going fuck you, over and over*, he says, untying the laces of my pants. He drags them down and his own quickly follow. He's so hard and swollen for me, all I want is to bring him inside me where he belongs. He must feel the hunger I'm feeling, because he gets a wicked grin. *And every time I do, I'm going to get all of my seed deep inside you. I'm going to work hard to put as many whelps in there as I possibly can.*

Oh. That wasn't what I expected. But as soon as he says it, I can feel the craving as deep in his soul as my own. I want to swallow him up and give him everything he wants. I'd never once thought of having a family, but raising little hellions with someone as loving and playful as Lo'zar would, perhaps, give me the thing I wish I'd always had.

I didn't know you could do that, I say. I try to imagine those children, and I raise an eyebrow. *Has anyone else done this before?*

He shrugs. *Who knows? Maybe we'll be the first.* He rubs the head of his cock on me, over my clit and around it, until I'm dripping onto the bed. Nodding with satisfaction, he starts to slowly slide inside, one soft, easy inch at a time. I feel my orgasm starting to build before he's even reached the innermost part of me, as he gently takes me.

By the time I'm crying out and wriggling underneath him, I'm a rigid coil of desire ready to burst open, and I want nothing more than to feel him unleash everything. Lo'zar leans down so his lips are on my earlobe, and breathes against me. "Rimi," he says, rolling my name over his tongue. *I'm going to give you all of it.*

I nod, and say his name back to him out loud, over and over. He gasps and sinks deep inside me, and then the dam breaks. I cry out, gripping him as tight as I can as he releases it all inside me, thrusting once more for good measure. When he's finished, Lo'zar wraps my legs tight around his waist and leans over me on his elbows.

There, he says with satisfaction. *I can't wait to see how big your tits get.*

Lo'zar! I bop him on the head. *You're not trying to get me pregnant just so my boobs are bigger, are you?*

No. Not just *because of that.* His smirk is so self-satisfied. *I also want to see you big and round with my whelps. I want to raise many smart, sweet ones. Just like you.*

I bury my face in his neck, trying to stifle the bright heat in my cheeks. I want that, too, whatever kind of life we end up with. I want to have children I can love, who would feel loved.

All right, big guy, I tell him. I can already feel his insatiable cock rousing itself again. *You'd better get to work.*

My charming troll grins down at me, mouth cocked to one side. *With pleasure.*

CHAPTER 25

Lo'zar

When we make landfall in Eyra Cove, I set out to learn who's in charge and where to find them. It's not hard to pick up a little thief sneaking around behind the shops. When I follow him into a dark alley and stop him, he's convinced I'm going to turn him in to the guards.

"Take me to your boss," I growl. "I want to speak to them."

I'm surprised to find not only is there an underbelly in Eyra Cove, but it's a mix of human and trollkin, too. I run a few small errands for the orcess who rules over the clan to prove I can be trusted. My sweet human mate is the perfect partner, standing prettily and making smalltalk with a merchant while I take what I need behind his back.

We never know where Gusak's eyes might be, so we stay hidden, too. It's good practice for Rimi, who has never learned to move quietly, without being seen. But she is light on her feet and her mind is always a step ahead of me, and it isn't long before we secure the big boss's interest. We have a talent, to walk the lines between human and trollkin, and that is invaluable to her.

Soon, I'm made aware of a shipment that needs to reach the human lands untaxed. After we talk it over, Rimi agrees that we should do it. I can wear the amulet, and she'll handle the communication. It's a good first test to see how she takes to it—a lifestyle of always moving, running missions that can sometimes be dangerous, and talking her way out of a pinch.

If I have to go be a farmer and wear this damn amulet every day, I'd do that for her. But I'd rather not.

We take a skiff, using my last necklace to barter, and head off into the channel. It's a difficult trip but we get to the other end, our cargo disguised with boxes of dry goods. Rimi talks to the guards at the docks in the human city, and even displays some of the fake cargo to convince them we're doing nothing untoward. We pass through without fuss, and take the river to the drop-off location.

The humans don't seem to mind that I'm mute, because Rimi is charming and beautiful and clearly quite good in her own language at saying what needs to be said. It helps immensely that we can communicate with one another in perfect silence, without anyone hearing us. We're paid well, and before we can decide where to go next, our contact asks if we can do some more work for them hauling rare artifacts. Rimi arches an eyebrow at me.

What do you think? she asks.

I think we should do it.

While we're out on the ocean, sitting side-by-side under a clear blue sky, Rimi picks through the crates of gems and sculptures and trinkets while I fall asleep to the sound of the lapping waves.

A short time later, though, Rimi taps me on the hand.

"Look." She's learned a little Trollkin, and I've picked up some

Freysian as we work, which comes in handy. There's a broken rock in her arms that looks like it was cracked off of a much bigger one. *Recognize this?*

She turns it so I can see the symbols carved into it: one half of a human's face and one half of a trollkin's, so close together their noses are almost touching. There doesn't appear to be any magic in it, but when she gives it to me to hold, the purple mist inside the amulet starts to glow.

Did we do what we were supposed to do? she asks me. *Whatever that pyramid was trying to tell us?*

I glance around at the open ocean, and listen to the peaceful squawk of distant seagulls.

I think so, I say. *But does it matter? I get to live my life with you. I don't care what some old rocks wanted.*

Rimi just laughs and shakes her head at me. *You wouldn't, would you?* She sits down beside me, taking my big, four-fingered hand in hers. We tap our fingers on the side of the boat, making a delightful little melody.

After a few runs like this, we're full up with coin and we've earned the trust of the human outlaws. We become their go-to for overseas transport, hauling all sorts of goods past tax collectors and inspectors. With our heads together, we are much too clever to get caught.

It's raining one day—pelting us, really—as we try to navigate our small skiff out of harm's way.

We need a bigger boat, Rimi says, out of seemingly nowhere.

Do we? This ship has been sufficient so far.

Something sturdier, she says. *More space.*

I think about this as the storm calms. When we're done putting the sails out, Rimi is breathing hard, and I help her sit down inside the cabin where it's dry.

Why is the boat not good enough all of the sudden? I ask. I know a little storm wouldn't rattle her, not after everything we've been through.

With a twitch of excitement, she scoots over to one side and invites me to sit down next to her. *Because there's going to be another person on board,* she says. *At least one.* She brings my hand to her chest, then drags it down until it's resting over her belly.

My heart leaps into my throat. *Is that so?* I lean down, pull up her shirt, and kiss her exposed stomach. So this is where my whelp will grow, big and strong.

It is so, she says with a giggle.

Whatever happens, I know they will have the most doting parents possible.

That night I take my mate slow and gentle, and she cries out underneath me until she's squeezing me so tight, I doubt if she'll ever let me go.

That would be quite all right with me.

Rimi

Once I'm so enormous I can't navigate the boat any longer, we set up camp not far from a human village, where we hired a midwife to help with the birth. The moment she sees me, she says, "Oh, there's two of them?"

Twins. That's why I'm full to popping, apparently. Every day Lo'zar plays with my breasts, licking them when they drip milk, and looking immensely pleased with himself.

But if there are going to be two of them, he says, sucking on my nipple, *where's mine?*

Lo'zar! I snort. *You can't get jealous of my tits. And you're the one who put those babies in there, by the way.*

He rubs his chin. *I guess I did. And I won't be happy until we have a whole clan.*

Going to start an organized criminal enterprise? I ask.

We could own the sea with just a horde of our children. He runs his hand down my rather enormous belly, ducking it between my legs. *You know, at our last stop, I overheard that there are others. Like us.*

Others? I'm not sure what he means.

Other pairs of human and trollkin.

I gasp as he runs his finger up and down me, testing how slick I am for him. *Really? So we aren't the only ones?*

I heard some live in Eyra Cove. A troll and a human, just like us.

Well, we must meet them, I say. *Maybe our strange children can be friends.*

He chuckles that boyish chuckle I love. *All right, my little mate. Perhaps you can find a friend, too.*

While we wait for the twins' arrival, Lo'zar sends a note to Graz, but we don't hear anything back. Perhaps that brilliant orc found what he was looking for, and decided not to return to Kalishagg— or he discovered some treasure even greater than we did.

When I finally go into labor, Lo'zar puts on the amulet to fetch the midwife, and I almost tear it off of him. I need him here, *my* troll. But when he holds my hand, looking into my eyes, I know that it's him.

After a day and a night, I'm drenched in my own sweat and exhausted all the way to my bones. Lo'zar's fallen asleep with his head on the bed when at last, I feel it. I'm finally almost there.

He jolts awake at my scream. "Fuck," he says, holding my hand tight. *I didn't know this was going to hurt you so much. I'm having second thoughts.*

You're having second thoughts now? I growl. He laughs, and then I'm lost to the pain.

Her scream pierces the air. I don't have to see her to know who she is, because I know her the way I know Lo'zar. But it's not over. He holds our screaming daughter, the tiny human girl with a thin coat of black hair on her head, while I pitch forward and cry out.

"He's not wanting to come out," the midwife says, trying to disguise her worry. "Just push harder, dear."

He isn't crying when he emerges, but the edges of my vision are already crawling in.

Is he breathing? I ask, terrified of the answer. Lo'zar is quiet for a long time as he holds our wailing daughter.

Eventually, he whispers the word, *Yes.*

Ji'zan is small, smaller than his sister, and quiet as a mouse. Lo'zar likes to curl up with him in the hammock, sometimes one in each arm, enjoying the ocean breeze. They're so tiny, our two little human children, that he can easily palm them.

It's so strange, he says, smoothing back Hara's hair, who's the much wilder of the two. *That they would come out human.* He shoots me a playful grin. *You didn't sleep around on me, did you?*

I tug on his braid as I sit in his lap, and he shifts to hold all three of us. *I wonder that, too,* I say, bringing Ji'zan into my arms. *I feel like it's tied to the pyramid, somehow. What we discovered down there.*

He cocks his head. *You think our whelps are magic?* It actually looks like he's considering this. *Bold statement. What's your evidence?*

I shrug. *Just a feeling.*

Suddenly, Lo'zar crows, "Oh!" and both Ji'zan and Hara start crying at once. I roll my eyes as he fishes around in his pocket for something—and pulls out two tiny gold rings.

What are those? I ask. *And when did you get them?*

Hey, I paid this time. He leans down and takes Hara's tiny hand, trying to put the ring on it. *Had them custom made.*

I carefully remove the ring. *Lo'zar. You can't give a ring to an infant.*

He frowns. *But it's insurance. Now they'll never know what it's like to have nothing.*

Tracing a finger down his tusk, I sigh and shake my head. *They'll never have nothing as long as they're with us. Don't worry.*

He looks at me in silence for so long, I wonder if time has frozen.

I'm so glad I found you, princess, he says, tucking a rogue hair behind my ear.

Even though we had to destroy a priceless artifact to get here? I ask.

No one was using it anyway.

The babies fall asleep again, rocked by the swaying of the boat.

I never think of my parents, not anymore. This is my world, my home, my place. And as long as Lo'zar and I are together, there's nothing we can't do.

THANK YOU FOR READING!

If you enjoyed this book, please consider leaving a review. Reviews are incredibly helpful for indie authors like me in reaching new readers!

Looking for the next Trollkin Lovers book?

Keeping the Human's Heart, an M/M/F story about two trollkin and one human woman, is now available!

Join My Newsletter!

For all the latest regarding books, and to get a FREE novella that takes place in the Trollkin Lovers universe, sign up for my newsletter!

www.LyonneRiley.com

For even more stories and lots of NSFW artwork, come check me out on Patreon!

www.Patreon.com/LyonneRiley

About the Author

Lyonne Riley published her first book at age five, which was written on tiny sheets of notebook paper, and she insisted on giving a copy to everyone she knew. She's been writing ever since, from fan fiction in her teen years to original fiction as an adult. After a stint in traditional publishing, she discovered what she truly wanted to write: very smutty stories about monstrous orcs and the little humans they worship.

Now she lives in the middle of nowhere with her dogs and spouse, writing sexy fairy tales.

facebook.com/lyonneriley

x.com/lyonneriley

instagram.com/lyonneriley

amazon.com/stores/Lyonne-Riley/author/B0C57K1NM3

Acknowledgments

I would like to thank everyone involved in helping me through the process of putting out this book. I can't say enough how much I appreciate the help and encouragement of the people around me—especially Amber, who told me I could do this in the first place.

Huge thank you to Rowan Woodcock for the gorgeous cover illustration. To my critique partners, Ash, Ruth, Kass, Emily and Cia, who gave me phenomenal feedback: You all make this possible. And of course, my amazing spouse, who has always supported my dreams—and given me lots of inspiration for my characters' sexy adventures.

I couldn't have done this without the expertise of my fellow self-published romance authors. Thank you for inviting me into your circles and helping me through this process.

And thank you to my readers, who gave this book a shot.

www.ingramcontent.com/pod-product-compliance
Lightning Source LLC
Chambersburg PA
CBHW071804190726